Hallmark
PUBLISHING

Dater's Handbook

Based on the Hallmark Channel Original Movie

Cara Lockwood

Hallmark
PUBLISHING

www.hallmarkpublishing.com
For more about the movie visit:
http://www.hallmarkchannel.com/daters-handbook

Table of Contents

One 5

Two 18

Three 30

Four 42

Five 50

Six 60

Seven 71

Eight 81

Nine 95

Ten 104

Eleven 113

Twelve 125

Thirteen 136

Fourteen 149

Fifteen 166

Sixteen 184

Seventeen 194

Eighteen 211

Nineteen 231

Twenty 242

Twenty-one 254

Epilogue 260

One

ARLY MORNING LIGHT CREPT OVER the snowcapped Rocky Mountains just as I hit mile three on my daily run down my favorite park trail, the crisp fall breeze cool across my face, my breath coming out in small, tiny puffs. Duke trotted beside me, his big pink tongue lolling out of his mouth, tail wagging as fast as his paws moved. He glanced up at me, loving this as much as I did. Duke was—hands down—the best golden retriever to ever live on this planet. Loyal, sweet, and he'd run longer than I did if I let him. I turned up REO Speedwagon on my ancient white iPod, a smile crossing my face as I mouthed the next line to "Can't Fight This Feeling."

Dated? Yep. Cheesy? Probably. But also *the most amazing band ever*? Truth. I challenge anyone to hear REO Speedwagon and *not* sing along. It's just not possible. I grew up with REO blaring in my parents' cars, and every time I heard them, it took me right back to that place, feet dangling in the backseat, the whole family singing as loudly as we could.

Peter—my, uh, boyfriend? He was odd with labels, so let's just call him the guy I'd been hanging out with for the last two years—always said I needed to get with the times. Ditch my iPod and 80s rock ballads. I liked them, though. They were comfortable, worn-in, familiar. They made me happy, and I knew better than anyone that happiness could disappear in an instant. I read somewhere once that the most fulfilled people were the ones who stopped and smelled the roses, the ones who accepted that sometimes life wasn't a bunch of breathtaking moments, but a whole bunch of little contented moments. Like running on my favorite trail, listening to my favorite band, with my favorite dog. My fitness watch beeped at me, announcing the fact that I'd hit 5K. I left the trail and climbed up on an outcropping of rocks, grinning. Duke hopped up with me, tongue out, panting. He knew the drill. We did this every time. I plucked the earbuds out of my ears because this show didn't need a soundtrack. Then, as if on cue, the sun came up from behind the Boulder foothills, breaking free of the highest peak, bathing the snow in warm, pink light.

"Now, look," I told Duke. "Isn't that gorgeous? I

mean, the mountains are pretty, sure, but even they need good lighting."

Duke blinked at me, not caring that I'd quoted my dad, something I'd been doing a lot lately. Probably because his birthday would have been this month— except he'd died ten years ago. My father had been one of my favorite people in the world, and then… overnight, he just…disappeared. Gone. No more corny jokes. No more lip-syncing to awesomely bad 80s music. No more big bear hugs.

I shook myself. *Sunrise, remember?* Gorgeous view, straight ahead. The kind of thing most everybody else just got to see in postcards and Sierra Club calendars. I had a front row view. I took another deep breath, the thin, cold air filling my lungs, already burning from the exercise. Who needed anything more than this? Seriously, though. Just breathe. This was all I needed. Or…maybe…someone to share it with. Someone other than a dog. I could call Peter, but he never got out of bed before ten. Owning a bar and managing it was a night gig. Besides, I knew already he didn't much care about nature, about *this.*

Duke whined, snapping me out of my nature-induced revelry. I glanced down at my golden retriever with his sad brown eyes, who sat still, patiently waiting. I knew what he wanted. The sunrise might be *my* favorite part of our daily ritual, but going off-leash was his. I stooped down and set him loose, letting him run the last twenty yards to the car, stopping to sniff every tree along the way.

As I opened the passenger side door, Duke leapt in, tag wagging. A good life that dog led, no question. I slid into the driver's seat and took one last look at the mountains ahead of me. The view this morning reminded me of a photograph my sister, Nadia, kept of our parents. It was taken long before they had us, but in it, they were sitting on a ledge, Rocky Mountains in the background, decked out in early '80s clothes. Mom wore acid-wash pleated jeans, with her hair frosted, and Dad sported a baseball shirt and bright white Nikes. Their faces told the story: so happy then, so in love.

I exhaled and instantly looked for something to do, a distraction from *feeling*. I didn't like the feels. Not when it came to sad things like Dad. I focused on fixing my dark ponytail, which was beginning to slide out of its tie. Then I started up the car and backed out of the spot. In a blink, we were at my condo. I pulled into the garage and let Duke lead me up the stairs by his leash to my loft, a recently renovated, completely Pottery Barn-furnished, two-bedroom condo I was insanely proud of. Never mind that I'd been living here four years already; I loved the dazzling white kitchen, the granite countertops, the wrap-around island, the gleaming pine floors, and the wood-burning fireplace. I bought this loft with my own money, money earned from my company, CB Branding. Every time I walked through my front door, I felt a little swell of pride.

I slipped inside, dropped my keys on my foyer table in the gleaming bowl, and let Duke off his leash.

"Go," I told him. "Go get your bone. Go get it!"

He trotted to his soft blue bed near the fireplace and grabbed an only slightly-chewed bone, wagging his tail.

"Good run today," I said. "Was that a 5K? Must be 35K in dog."

I poured myself a glass of water and filled Duke's bowl. I sipped and opened my laptop to stream the morning news, hoping for a quick check of the weather before I showered. The perky hosts of *Wake Up Denver* were in full chatty mode this morning, sitting behind their silver half-circle desk, the orange show logo emblazoned on the front and a happy sun peeking over a blue mountaintop. Behind the hosts stretched the beautiful Rocky Mountains, bathed in sunlight.

"Welcome back to *Wake Up Denver*!" chirped the middle-aged host, Kyle, wearing another one of his basic bland suits that somehow managed to match his perfect salt-and-pepper, pre-Just-For-Men look. "If you're not quite up yet, this next segment is sure to get your blood pumping."

I raised an eyebrow at Duke. Kyle *always* said this or something like it, no matter what the segment. He was either running out of things to say in the morning or easily excitable.

Kyle's co-host, Cissy Cho, smiled at the camera, her sleek black hair perfectly straight and gleaming. "Stopping by to visit with us today is none other than Dr. Susie," she said. "The best-selling author of *What's Wrong with Mr. Right* and *Checklist for Love*. Dr. Susie will talk to us about her current release, *The Dater's Handbook*—a how-to guide for the modern single gal."

Ugh. *Modern single gal?* What was this? 1945? Anytime I heard the word "gal," I always thought of black-and-white, Humphrey Bogart movies with plucky sidekick heroines who wore pencil skirts with suit jackets and hats, and were always called "spunky." So, obviously, Cissy had hooked me. Now I had to watch this next segment for entertainment value alone.

Though, technically, I wasn't a single gal, spunky or no. I had...Peter. He owned his own bar, and worked out nearly every day—he could bench-press me in a pinch. He was all man. Nobody would ever accuse him of being too sensitive or in touch with his feelings. But who wanted that? Not me. Conversations about the *L-word* gave me the willies. My older sister, Nadia? She'd discuss relationships all day. I'd rather make a joke than get into anything serious.

Peter was perfect for that. He never dissected his emotions, and that meant I never had to delve into mine. It was, in many ways, a perfect relationship, though Peter would be the very first to tell me I shouldn't call it that. "Relationship" was one of many labels he hated. Just like "girlfriend" and "boyfriend," other labels he despised. But then he'd always say, "Why put love in box? Why put a label on it?" It was what it was.

During the commercial break, I went about trying to figure out what to have for breakfast. *I should drink a healthy, yogurt-blueberry smoothie.* But what I really wanted to do was head to the coffee shop a half block away and grab two chocolate croissants and a pumpkin spice scone. I sighed. No. *Today*, I'd have self-control. *Today*, I'd not cave in to the cravings and pretty much undo all the good I did running the trail this morning. I had a sweet tooth, courtesy of Mom, that acted more like a sweets monster. It demanded endless icing-crusted, gooey chocolate sacrifices all day long.

No. Blueberries. Yogurt. Blender. Nothing chocolatey or carb heavy. I nodded, determined, as I packed the blender and made a healthy, low-cal, low-carb, no-processed-sugar breakfast. I took a drink, trying hard to tell myself this was just as good as a gooey chocolate croissant right from the convection oven. The show came back as I sipped the smoothie, my inner sweets monster not the least bit satisfied. I tried to ignore its grumblings as I glanced at the screen and saw the camera pan out to Dr. Susie. She was blonde, well put together, mid-forties, not an eyelash out of place. She probably never fought cravings for a chocolate croissant. I bet she was a strict kale-lemon juice smoothie kind of woman. Maybe she knew something I didn't.

Cissy, the host, held up a copy of *The Dater's Handbook.*

"Dr. Susie, I've read your new book and I love it," Cissy gushed. "But for our audience members who haven't, why are so many women having issues finding the right men in today's dating world?"

Dr. Susie smiled, as if she were a teacher about to impart wisdom on her young charges. "Well, like with most issues in life, the first step is admitting that you have a problem. In this case, it may be hard to admit but…" Dr. Susie turned her attention to the camera, and it felt like she was talking right to me. "Ladies, the problem is not the *men* in your life. It's you."

Me? What was she talking about? *I* was just fine.

But Dr. Susie wasn't finished. "You're picking the rebel guy, the fun guy, the deep brooding artist—"

I thought of Peter and nearly choked on my smoothie. There wasn't really anything brooding or artistic about him. He was a jock, through and through, but I liked that about him. He was simple.

"When what you really need is someone reliable, dependable, responsible."

"Reliable, dependable and responsible," I mimicked, and then I glanced at Duke. "Sounds like they're talking about you." Duke cocked his head, as if to tell me I'd left something out. "But they forgot about loyal." He seemed satisfied by that, and I bent down and scratched him behind the ears. I finished my smoothie and glanced at the clock. Time for a shower or I'd be late for work.

I arrived at my office with a little extra bounce in my step. I loved coming to work every day in the tchotchkes company I'd built from scratch. I might not be promoting world peace, but I sure as heck was plastering logos on foam stress balls, water bottles, and reusable tote bags. My phone rang before I was even to the elevator, and I recognized the number of a potential client I'd been trying to land for weeks. Bob Meister owned a national chain of grocery stores.

"Bob!" I clicked on my hands-free set as I swished by the security desk in the lobby and waved to the guard. "Thanks so much for calling me back. So, here's the capsule pitch for your logo..." The elevator doors shut, but thankfully, my cell reception held. "Think about this: every day, millions of fans fill stadiums doling out their hard-earned money on their favorite beverage. And—"

The elevator doors opened on my office floor and I stepped out, heading to the two glass doors of my office where I employed about thirty people. I headed down the samples hallway, happy to see everything in place, all the shelving and cubicles immaculate, just the way I liked them, and of course, straight ahead, the wall of windows looking out at the Rockies. That view was why I'd picked this building for our headquarters. When I stared at that window, I thought about Dad, the man who'd told me when I was twelve that I should be my own boss one day.

"We advertise in ballparks already, Cass," Bob said. I knew this, as he'd taken real estate right behind home plate at Coors Field, where the Denver Rockies play.

Dana, my perky and sweet-as-pie assistant, met me in the hallway to grab my workbag as she handed me a cup of piping hot coffee. What would I do without Dana? She was a bright-eyed, enthusiastic blonde who anticipated my needs before I even knew about them.

I focused on the phone and Bob as I headed to my office in the corner. I snagged a red Solo cup from the shelf nearby and glanced at it for inspiration.

"Yes, but, Bob, they look inside their cup, and

they see nothing. Six inches of blank plastic." I walked past a wall of our sample merchandise, logoed stadium foam fingers, cups, napkins, pens, notepads, footballs, and neatly folded T-shirts and sweatshirts. "But what they could be seeing is your company's logo, Bob. This is *prime* advertising space, and you will be the first to claim it."

"Hey... I never thought about that." Bob considered this a moment. I could almost feel him imagining *Robert's Superstore* in front of hundreds of thousands of new eyeballs. "That's a good idea."

Oh, I know it is. Almost got him...and...

"I'm in," he said.

Got him.

"That's terrific, Bob. We can print your logo on the cups and have them shipped out on..."

Dana, who had been hanging on my every word, tapped on her iPad. "Wednesday, the fifteenth," she said.

"Friday, the seventeenth," I told Bob.

"Invoice me, and we'll get this started," he said.

"We'll send you a confirmation by email. Thank you so much for your business. We appreciate it." I did a little celebration dance on the inside. That deal could be huge!

Dana quirked her head to one side, and I realized she didn't know why I put off the delivery order by two days.

"We'll ship them on Wednesday and he'll love us," I said. "Can you make sure first thing Monday morning, we email those graphics?"

"Okay." Then Dana froze. "Oh…uh… No." Dana frowned, uncharacteristic of her normally bubbly nature. "Uh, actually, Cass, Monday doesn't work for me." She waved her left hand at me, and the office light glinted on her giant diamond engagement ring.

Ugh! That's right. Dana was getting married on Saturday and planned to jet off to her honeymoon next week.

"How could I forget? Yes! It's your big weekend!"

Dana literally looked like she might burst with happiness—literally burst.

"Okay, *fine*, go abandon me and live happily ever after." I took her hands and grinned. If anyone deserved a happily-ever-after, it was Dana.

Dana pointed at the deliciously happy smile on her face. "I can't stop doing this. I've tried! I can't. I'm getting married! I'm going to be Mrs. Dana Schmointz!" Dana stomped her feet in a little celebratory dance and then let out a high-pitched squeal so intense it hurt my ears.

"Mrs. Sch-moi-ntz," I sounded out, trying to seem excited about the name but failing. I almost wanted to tell her she should consider keeping her maiden name, Abrams. It's *way* less goofy than Schmointz, which, let's be honest, sounds like Schmuck.

Dana missed my lack of enthusiasm, as she was wrapped up in her own. She let out another yelp of joy.

"Okay," I said, and she grabbed my hands and bounced up and down, and we both did a little dance in the office before she calmed down a bit.

"I hate to even ask this." Her face still beamed with uncontrollable happiness. "But did you decide on the...you know..." She appeared a little uncomfortable now. "The plus one?"

It was then that I remembered I hadn't exactly, one hundred percent gotten Peter to agree to go with me... yet.

"I am so sorry. I am the worst wedding guest ever," I said. "Peter's just not..." I was about to say "that into weddings," but looking at Dana's beaming face, I couldn't even get the words out. Why spoil her good mood? Besides, it would be like I was speaking another language. "It's a busy season at the bar, and he's not one hundred percent sure he's got all shifts covered. Can I tell you...tomorrow?"

"Of course. Seriously, I hate to even ask. Really, it's no trouble." Dana bopped away, humming. I'd need to figure out if I did have a plus one or not, tonight, when I saw Peter at the bar. The last time we'd talked about it, he'd said "maybe," and I needed to turn that maybe into a yes.

Two

"SCHMOINTZ? SHE'S SERIOUSLY TAKING HIS last name?" my sister Nadia said as I sat with her and her husband Michael at Peter's bar, Sportz, that night.

Michael sipped at his beer. "No hyphen?"

Nadia continued, amazed. "What kind of name is Schmointz, anyway?"

"An absolutely hilarious one," Michael said and took another long swig. My brother-in-law had the driest sense of humor and happened to be one of the most patient men to ever live, which was why he tolerated my sister's regular freakouts. Don't get me wrong. Nadia is a wonderful, smart, and funny woman, but she's also so Type A that she makes me look like a slacker. When we were kids, she refused to let me touch anything when we had tea parties. Everything had to be set up to her exact specifications, from the tiny plastic spoon to the miniature sugar bowl next to Mr. Giggles, the bear.

Little had changed now that she was married and staying at home with my four-year-old nephew, Jeremy. She was the kind of mom who spent hours reading every bit of developmental research she could get her hands on, fretting about everything that could go wrong—from GMOs to childhood cancer. Now that she and Michael were expecting Baby Number Two, I'd wondered if she'd loosen her grip a little bit, but so far, I hadn't seen any signs. She even had a binder filled with possible baby names—boy, girl, and neutral, listed alphabetically—sitting on her dining room table at home.

"She was just so happy," I said, glancing at my own beer in front of me at the narrow high-top table. "I don't think I've ever seen anyone that excited about anything. Ever. I didn't even know people got that excited."

"Of *course,* she's excited. Marrying Schmointz is her fairy-tale dream," said the woman who, before she had a binder for baby names, cherished her binder filled with bridal gowns and flower arrangements.

"It's kind of like our wedding, right, honey?" Michael piped in. "A fairy tale. A dream."

"Dream wasn't the word." Nadia sipped at her cranberry juice with a hint of soda water as she rested her hand on her now protruding belly. "More like…"

"Nightmare?" I offered.

"The word was *nauseous*," Nadia said. "I tried to run…then I threw up." She glanced at me.

"She's not kidding, because I had to hold the veil," I said. Ugh. That was a memory I'd rather soon forget. I'd been crammed into the tiny bathroom at the church, desperately trying to keep the tulle out of the line of fire.

"You're such a good sister," she said, and we exchanged a look. *Oh, I know I am.* Michael chuckled to himself into his beer, but that's probably because even he had no idea how close he'd come to *not* marrying my sister that day. Nadia, the girl who'd dreamed of her wedding day her whole life, had suddenly gotten a horrible case of cold feet the very night before. I'd had to talk her out of running for the hills. Michael was a goofball, but he was a stand-up guy, and he loved my sister. And now look at her, happy—mostly—with baby number two on the way.

I'd done my good deed that day.

I glanced at the empty seat next to me and again wondered where Peter was. I knew he oversaw the bar and couldn't spend the whole evening chatting with us, but he'd almost entirely ignored us since we came in. I'd gotten a quick wave and a hold-on-a-minute sign. That had been twenty minutes ago. I guessed they might be understaffed tonight. I didn't see the usual number of waitresses. Peter always seemed to lose employees. People quit or just didn't show up—one of the dangers of running a sports bar. I liked that Peter owned his own business. We bonded over being entrepreneurs. He understood the stress of meeting payroll and trying to find good employees. Besides, I thought he'd been smart to roll over his money from playing baseball for the Rockies into a place that could build him a stable financial future.

I had to admit I liked telling people I was dating a semi-famous person, even if "dating" might not have been the right word for it. Peter seemed fine with hanging with my sister and Michael—usually because they picked up the tab when they took us out to eat—but he'd yet to go deeper and meet my mom or my friends. Even after two years, I honestly couldn't say if I was his standing Saturday night date or not. But I decided not to push it. I hated relationship talks.

I saw Peter near the kitchen doors now, holding a platter of wings and talking to a group of girls wearing Rockies shirts. I told myself he was only being a good bar owner, making sure his customers were having a good time. Yet, why did he linger so long at *their* table, near the girl with the low-cut shirt who seemed to be flipping her blonde hair constantly? Why didn't he give any love to the high top of dudes right nearby? Peter must have felt me looking, because he eventually dragged himself away from the pretty blonde. He grinned as he headed to our table, carrying an oversized platter of wings.

"Oh, look. Here's your boyfriend, bearing gifts," Michael said, perking up at the sight of food.

Peter looked like the professional baseball player he used to be: tall and broad, with a killer smile and amazing blue eyes. He was part overgrown frat boy, part jock, and all confidence. Everything about Peter seemed beefy, from his thick, muscled shoulders to his extensively worked calves. I had to admit that watching him cross the bar wasn't a bad way to spend the night.

"You guys have to try these," Peter said, placing the tray on our high-top table. "Cilantro Sesame-Honey wings."

I glanced at the sauce-covered chicken and frowned. I was allergic to honey. Peter knew this. I'd told him *many* times. Like when he tried to feed me honey-mustard sauce. That time he drizzled honey on my waffles. That other time he dumped honey in my chamomile tea when I was sick and I got, well...even sicker. Honey causes my tongue to swell and my throat to close up, and if I don't get an EpiPen shot, then it's a trip to the emergency room.

Nadia looked at the plate in front of us as if it was full of live bees.

Peter grinned at me, still not getting the message I

was trying to silently drill into his brain. "And since I can't hang with you because we're shorthanded, they're on the house."

Michael grabbed one. "Well, you know I love free," he said. Nadia, meanwhile, swiped the food from his hand.

I cleared my throat, but Peter just looked at me blankly. He seriously did not remember.

"You know I love wings," I said and clutched his arm—his big, bulky, muscular arm. "But I can't have them because…" I paused to give him time to catch up. I really didn't want to have to finish my sentence and remind him of the honey allergy—again. Especially not in front of Nadia. She was already *not* all that impressed with Peter. She'd told me so.

But Peter just stared at me, blue eyes vacant. He wasn't getting it. I continued. "Because of the…" Another pause, another blank stare from him. "The honey?"

I expected a burst of recognition, a sheepish apology. Yet still, he seemed befuddled. Okay, so I got that Peter wasn't the sharpest knife in the drawer, but did he really not remember?

"Duh," Nadia piped in, glaring as only my sister can. "She's allergic?"

Michael took a second bite of his wing, happy to stay out of this awkward moment.

I studied Peter, who somehow *still* managed to look blank. Maybe blank was his resting face. Maybe blank was just *what he was all the time.* He really hadn't remembered, not even after two years, not even after Nadia had flat out reminded him. And even now, as he glanced at the table, I knew he probably would forget again, too.

Normally, I liked the fact that Peter wasn't too into my business, wasn't too clingy or needy, but in this very moment, when he nearly fed me a food that could kill me, I thought maybe I needed to rethink that. If he couldn't recall basic details about me—life-saving details—then did he really care about me at all?

We had a no-fuss, no-muss kind of relationship, but shouldn't he know me well enough by now to avoid a trip to the ER?

Michael took a third bite of chicken wing then and coughed, his excitement about finishing the wing suddenly abating as the seasoning finally hit him. "Interesting…" he murmured, frowning. "Uh, yeah… They're interesting." Clearly, the cilantro-honey failed to impress. Peter, however, missed the tepid compliment and just beamed with pride.

"Yeah…interesting." Nadia frowned at the wing in her hand and then dropped it, clearly uninterested in finishing.

"Tangy?" Michael offered, but also slowly set the

food back on his plate. That meant the things had to be darn near inedible. Michael ate nearly everything.

Peter was always trying weird recipes he found online. He believed he might really have a knack for cooking, and I never had the heart to tell him that wasn't his strong suit. Come to think of it, what *was* his strong suit? Having a strong jaw? A killer smile?

"So, here's what I'm thinking about tomorrow, guys," Peter said, clapping his hands in boyish excitement. "The college game starts at eleven tomorrow. We get some subs, gather round the big screen and—boom!—football marathon."

"We are so in!" Michael declared, grinning. Nadia glared at him, giving his shin a nudge under the table.

"We have two birthday parties tomorrow," she reminded him.

"We are so out," Michael said, crestfallen.

I had to bite my tongue. I'd told Peter about Dana's wedding tomorrow. Yes, he'd said he hated weddings, but I thought I'd maneuvered him to more of a "maybe, we'll see" kind of place. But now it seemed as if he didn't remember having a conversation about it at all. First, the honey, then totally spacing on Dana's wedding?

"So?" Peter asked me.

"And...we have Dana's wedding?" I quirked an

eyebrow. *Remember? That wedding you said, "maybe" you'd "think about"?*

"You know how I feel about weddings." Peter sighed. He shook his head slowly as if *I* was the one who'd dropped the ball.

Yes, but... You said, "Maybe." You said, "Maybe it won't be all that bad." But before I could remind him of this little detail, Michael jumped in. "Wait. You're not going to the wedding?" He studied Peter, amazed.

"I don't do weddings." Peter shook his head. Now I realized that all the *maybes* and *we'll sees* were just polite ways of saying no. I hadn't actually been changing his mind at all. He'd been determined to decline the invite the entire time.

"And you're okay with that?" Michael stared at me now, blinking.

No, I'm not okay with that, I want to say.

"Yes," I said, unable to keep the sarcasm out of my voice. "I mean, I can't ask him to miss the games. That are on *every week.* That would be selfish of me."

Peter missed the sarcasm. He nodded his head, relieved. I used to think it was kind of cute that he missed sarcasm. But lately...even his muscled, broad shoulders and dimpled smile weren't enough to distract me from his other shortcomings.

"Seriously?" Michael was aghast now, glancing

back and forth between the two of us. "How do you get out of these things?"

I knew he was thinking about the two kids' birthday parties he had to go to tomorrow. I was sure he would rather be watching college football.

"It's easy." Peter shrugged one meaty shoulder. "Weddings are boring to everyone except the two people getting married."

I mean, sure, we'd both agreed that most weddings were a waste of time. If I really searched my feelings, deep down, did I want to spend a whole Saturday night watching Dana stare dreamily into the eyes of her Mr. Schmointz?

Uh, probably not.

But that wasn't the point, really. I had to go. Dana wasn't only my best employee, she was also one of my best friends. And Peter should do this for me because it was important.

Michael looked astounded. "Yeah, but…that's what couples do. They do boring things together."

I wasn't sure if Nadia thought that was sweet, insulting, or both, but in any case, she stayed quiet. She studied me, and I could almost read her mind. *Told you Peter's the wrong guy for you.*

"We do plenty of boring things together," Peter admitted. "Just not weddings."

"Or family functions," I blurted. "Or work events. Or—"

"That's because," Peter said, cutting me off. "Whenever you go to those functions, everyone asks you 'so when is it your turn?' It's so annoying, right?"

"I wouldn't know," I said, trying to be flippant, airy. "I've never heard anyone ask me that about us."

Nadia arched an eyebrow at me from across the table, and in that small gesture lay a novel's worth of commentary. I realized in that moment, that it was true. No one had ever asked me when I was going to take it "to the next step" with Peter. Most people just plastered neutral smiles on their faces when I even mentioned Peter—which, come to think of it, wasn't that often. And the idea of actually taking the next step—whatever that might mean—with Peter... Well, did I even want to do that?

He grinned at me. "They don't ask about us because we avoid those types of situations. See? It all works." He clapped me on the back almost like I was a teammate, not his girlfriend. An uncomfortable silence descended on our little table, which Peter, of course, failed to notice. Peter glanced up and eyed the cute girls in the Rockies jerseys across the bar once more, but then his attention settled back on me.

"Hey, I'll get you some more wings," Peter said, backing away from our table. "Ah! But this time... *no* honey." He aimed a finger gun at me, and I managed a weak smile.

"Ah! Now who's thinking?" Michael piped in, pointing at Peter as if he'd just hit a home run. Once Peter ambled out of earshot, Michael leaned over the table to my sister. "Are they a couple or not?" he asked in the loudest whisper I'd ever heard.

"I'm right here," I said, glancing down at the enormous plate of honey-doused wings at the center of the table. Well, on the bright side, I guessed Dana officially had her answer about my RSVP: no plus-one for me.

Three

I HARDLY THOUGHT ABOUT PETER THE next day as I sat through the wedding ceremony, a truly touching exchange of vows beneath the white chuppah, as Dana Abrams officially became Mrs. Dana Schmointz. Now I understood what people meant by the phrase "beaming with happiness" because afterward, Dana looked like she could light up the night sky with her smile. The guests gathered in the immense ballroom of the swanky hotel in downtown Denver as we all dutifully plucked our seating cards from the table where they were arranged. I glanced around the beautifully decorated reception, my attention lingering on the dessert table, where the impressive three-layer cake towered over other smaller slices of vanilla and chocolate goodness. My inner sweets monster reared its head, and I had to fight it back down. *In good time,* I told it. *In good time.*

I searched for my seat at number five, but when I found it, I wished I hadn't. It was, quite literally, the kids' table. I recognized the flower girl and ring bearer from the ceremony, but I didn't know the other children. I saw two empty chairs and had a horrifying thought: what if Dana had left that spot open? What if it was just going to be me and a bunch of kids who could barely be called tweens?

Before I could descend into full-blown panic mode, I glanced up and saw a man in a gray suit and lavender tie approach. Clean-cut and attractive, he wore his dark hair swept back and bore a cocksure grin on his face. He hadn't noticed me yet. He focused on the flower girl in the pale pink dress.

"Uh-oh," he said, standing near one of two empty chairs. "Table five? Just the *best* table in the entire place, am I right?" The man slid into the empty seat next to the flower girl. "Are you kids ready to get this party started? First thing we're going to do is order a full round of Shirley Temples, on me. Who's with me?"

He offered the flower girl a high five, and she smacked his palm. A cheer went up from the group. He had quite obviously won over the mini crowd. He was so sweet, I couldn't help but be impressed. I knew Peter wouldn't have even tried. He didn't like kids and made his dislike known on a regular basis.

"You're one cool dude," the flower girl said, echoing

my thoughts. The stranger looked up then and caught my eye. I held the card for table five in my hand, and he smiled at me. I felt a warm little glow in the pit of my stomach. Maybe this reception wouldn't be a disaster, after all. I scooted over to the empty chair. He pushed it back for me and I took a seat.

"Hello," he said. "Welcome to table five, the best table at the wedding. Would you like to join us in a round of Shirley Temples? Miss…" He glanced at the place card in my hand. "Miss Cassandra Brand?"

"Uh…Cass, actually, and that sounds lovely, Mr…" He held up his card and I read it. "Mr. Zappia."

"Robert Zappia." He offered his hand and I shook it, the warmth of his big palm covering mine. *Strong hands*, I thought, suddenly enjoying a little jolt at the connection. He had puppy-dog brown eyes that never left mine.

"Make it a double, Mr. Zappia," I joked, and he laughed, a warm, gooey laugh that I almost felt in the tips of my toes. Robert's eyes grew big, and he made faces at the children at the table.

"She's going crazy, kids!" he declared and some of them giggled.

Upbeat accordion music began playing, and the groom, Jim, came to tap Robert on the shoulder. "Time to dance," he told Robert, and Dana motioned me up, too. People stood and began clapping along to the traditional Horah dance as we all formed circles on the dance floor. The flower girl, I noticed, slipped right beside Robert but he reached out for me, clasping my hand.

I had to admit, I didn't mind the contact. His hand pressed against mine, warm and protective. He smiled at me once more, brown eyes sparkling, as we danced our way in a circle to the beat. Groomsmen brought chairs, and suddenly, the crowd lifted the bride high in the air as Robert and I moved to the side. We still kept time, clapping with the beat, but even the music couldn't drown out Dana's glee as they raised her up and she declared, "Can you believe it? I'm married! I'm officially Mrs. Dana Schmointz!" Then she let out a long, joyful shout that people probably heard in Idaho.

Robert glanced down at me, eyebrow raised. "Can you believe it?" he murmured, imitating Dana. I had to laugh as I let out a high-pitched squeal of my own, and Robert did, too, as a waiter came by and offered us flutes of champagne.

Oh, I liked Robert more by the minute.

I took a glass of bubbly and then made my way back to the table, a little out of breath from dancing in heels. Robert followed me, and we sat in our seats, the chairs around us mostly empty, the kids off somewhere else.

"You dance a mean Horah," Robert told me, clinking his champagne flute against mine. I laughed.

"Well, thank you. You dance a pretty mean Horah

yourself, Mr. Zappia." Despite only knowing him a hot five minutes, I felt relaxed with him. There was something conspiratorial in the way he looked at me, something I liked.

The waiters came and served dinner, and as we ate, we chatted. He'd met the happy couple in college, and he told me how meeting Dana had changed Jim's life for the better. I told him about Dana, and how Jim had changed her life, as well—and everybody else's in the office, since we'd all been subject to the high-pitched squeals of happiness since they'd gotten engaged.

A few more couples whirled on the dance floor.

"They look like they're having fun," he said, taking a sip of his champagne.

"It's great, but dancing is only the second-best part of a wedding."

"What, pray tell, is the first-best thing?" Robert leaned in, and I became hyper aware of how broad his shoulders were, how low his voice. I leaned in, too, and I inhaled the scent of his aftershave, something spicy and sweet with just the hint of vanilla. The man smelled good.

"The cake—clearly!" I'd been eyeing that beautifully frosted beast from across the room since I'd gotten here. I eyed a waiter that delivered a piece of that deliciousness to the table next to us. When was it *our* turn?

"Speaking of cake…" Robert turned to our left, and we saw Dana and her new husband feeding each other frosted bites. Lucky ducks. "They really are the perfect couple."

It was obvious how happy they were—sickeningly happy. I thought of my parents for a moment, back when Mom and Dad used to sneak kisses in the kitchen when they thought we weren't looking. Nadia and I always found it so gross, so icky, and Nadia asked often why they couldn't be like *other* parents, the ones who could—and did—keep their hands off one another. Nadia liked to tell them they were ruining us for any hope of a real relationship as adults. Because, after all, what chance did we have of finding what they had? We all knew relationships like that were as rare as a perfect diamond.

My stomach tightened, as it did every time I thought about Dad.

"Yeah," I said, shrugging. "If you're into that I'm-going-to-be-so-happy-for-the-rest-of-my-life thing.'"

"Yeah, who wants that?" Robert joked along with me. "Blech. BOR-ing."

"Boring!" I echoed and laughed a little. Boy, I could stare at those brown eyes all night. Handsome didn't begin to cover it, but there was something else there, too. A playfulness, maybe? I'd forgotten what playful was like. Peter wasn't playful. He was almost always serious.

Robert's expression grew somber. "But, seriously, people want love." The way he said it made me think he was talking about himself. "They want the happily-ever…"

He mimed screaming and then added, "Aaaaafter!"

I joined him in the mock scream.

Peter would never have admitted that men want happily-ever-afters. He'd once said men only want *happily-right-now.* But talking about forever love seemed a tad too close to talking about feelings. I itched to change the subject. I glanced up to try to find the waiters with the cake. Where *were* they?

As if hearing my inner cry, the waiter came and plunked down a piece of cake in front of the nine-year-old flower girl who'd just materialized from wherever she'd been hiding, as if she, too, had a second sense for dessert.

"Hey, kiddo," Robert said as the waiter served him next.

"Oh, that looks really good," I said, realizing the waiter had to go back for more cake. Those were his last two servings. Come on, couldn't he see I was dying for cake over here? My sweets monster was literally having a fit. It looked so good, too. Delicious buttercream icing over…was that white cake or… I needed to know. *Now.* I grabbed my fork and sunk it into the delicious, sweet goodness. The bite was in my mouth before I even had time to think about how rude it might be.

"Put the cake on the table and the kids run back..." Robert said, trailing off when he saw the missing bite out of his cake. "Excuse me. That's *my* cake, woman."

"Mmmmm..." I murmured, stolen bite still melting on my tongue. I should've felt badly about it, but, honestly, the cake was just astounding—buttercream, vanilla-y yumminess. "It's soooo good." I grinned. Besides, something about pushing Robert's buttons just felt fun.

The server returned and plopped my own piece of cake in front of me. *Geez—finally!*

"Turn about!" He moved his fork into my cake's airspace. Instinctively, I rose to defend what was mine. I put the tongs of my fork on the back of his hand.

"Uh-uh," I growled, pushing him away from my cake. The flower girl burst out laughing.

"Do you see what's going on here?" Robert asked her.

The girl nodded, the ring of blooms in her hair bobbing. "Yeah, she just stole your cake!"

I gobbled the rest of my dessert down in no time, trying not to notice that I'd beaten even the kids at the table. *Darn you, inner sweets monster.* I finished the last of my champagne and then excused myself so I could head to the restroom. Once inside the ladies' room, I re-applied my lipstick and smoothed down my dark hair in the mirror. I considered the fact that, shockingly, I wasn't having a terrible time. I knew that had everything to do with Robert, whose quick wit had made the evening fly by.

I missed that with Peter. He didn't do flirty banter. Heck, he didn't do *banter,* period. Sure, he had a fantastic body and chiseled good looks, but where did that get you if you had no good inside jokes?

I left the bathroom, and the first thing I saw was Robert waltzing with the flower girl on the dance floor. She stood on his feet as he moved her slowly in circles. *Adorable.* His back was to me, but I was close enough to overhear him tell her, "You are a wonderful dancer."

"Thank you," the flower girl said but then wrinkled her nose. "You're a little clunky."

I put my hand over my mouth to stifle a laugh. That girl was a walking truth bomb.

"Wow, thanks," Robert said, acting hurt. "That's because you're stepping on my toes." He reached down and picked her up as if the nine-year-old weighed nothing. Strong arms, I noticed. And it was sweet how he twirled her around.

"Are you going to ask that lady out on a date?" the girl asked him.

I ducked behind a pillar just as the pair moved closer to me.

"Do you think I should?" Robert asked the girl. I peeked around the column, not sure what I should do. My churning stomach told me fleeing was good. Yet, I wanted to hear what he'd say.

"You want to get married before you're too old and crinkly, don't you?"

"First off, you have to go on a couple of dates first and then you get married," Robert told her. "That's how it works."

Sage advice.

"Well, you two are cute together. Especially when she tried to stab you with her fork. That was funny."

"Funny?" Robert pretended to be upset. "Glad it made *you* laugh."

I grinned, remembering the look of mock outrage on Robert's face. He was a good sport, I had to give him that. I was *not* such a good sport when people tried to steal my dessert.

The girl cocked her head to one side. "You'd better ask her out before someone else does and she gets married."

Robert put the girl down on the floor. "You, kiddo, are right," he said, and my heart jumped a little. He knelt in front of the girl and tapped her softly on the nose. "You are so right. Wish me luck." He moved away from her to cross the dance floor. "And thank you for my dance!"

I swallowed hard. I knew Robert and I flirted most of the night, but I never thought it might end in an actual date. After all, I had that thing Peter didn't want to label going on. For two years! It meant something, even though I wasn't sure what. Accepting a date with Robert would be wrong, wouldn't it? But then, did I want to have to tell him and those intelligent dark eyes no?

Someone tapped the microphone onstage and then I saw Jim and Dana standing there, holding hands.

"And now, the time has come for the traditional throwing of the dead flowers," he announced to the crowd as Dana elbowed him, a grin on his face. "Bouquet time! All you single ladies gather round— over by the DJ!"

As Dana stepped off the stage, smiling at me and pointing, I felt a bit of panic well up in my throat. Dana would no doubt aim that toxic bouquet at me. And then what? I'd go show Peter the flowers and tell him, "It's our turn"? The thought made me light-headed and nauseated. And what about Robert? What would I tell him if he asked me out?

Ugh. This was my cue to leave. I glanced over at the coat check and raced to it, grabbing my jacket from the rack and slinging it on. I managed to run up to Dana just before she reached the DJ.

She saw my jacket, and a tiny worry line creased

her temple. "You're going?" she asked me. "But you're not going to stay for the flowers?" She held up her bouquet, and the look of disappointment on her face told me all I needed to know: she had planned to launch them at me.

"Sorry, I just..." I glanced at Robert, who glanced around the room, most likely looking for me. "I can't stay," I said, shaking my head. "But you're the most beautiful bride I've ever seen. You and Jim are wonderful together, and I'm so very happy for you."

The crush of bridesmaids and other singletons crowded impatiently over by the DJ, and I knew I couldn't keep Dana a second longer.

"Congratulations again!" I said and hugged my assistant. She squeezed me back and then Jim swept her off to do her bridal-bouquet-tossing duties.

I stepped out into the cold fall air and sighed, my breath escaping in a white cloud as I headed to my car, parked in the lot around the corner. I thought again about Robert. *I really should tell him good-bye.*

Then again, no, I shouldn't. Better me sneaking out than having to tell him no if he asked me out. But I knew things had already gone too far. I'd *let* them go too far. I picked up my pace and my heels clacked on the sidewalk as I zipped up my jacket and headed to my car.

Four

MOM, NADIA AND I SAT together at the coffee shop in the suburbs the next day, all staring appreciatively at the trio of delectable desserts we'd ordered to share. This was what we did on Sundays. Some families brunched, but we had coffee and dessert. Every Sunday. Or, really, as often as we could. Outside, the wall of the Rocky Mountains stood as our backdrop as we sat by the wood-burning fireplace in the nook, sharing double chocolate cake and peanut butter and marshmallow brownies, and a strawberry cheesecake.

I should've been having *none* of these, considering how much cake I ate at the wedding the night before, but when I was with Mom, there was no denying our mutual inner sweets monsters. Even Nadia, who was better at keeping the monster at bay than the two of us, indulged with unusual ferocity today. No doubt because she was having dessert for two.

Mom stabbed the double chocolate with her fork and took a hearty bite. "Mmmm," she said, eyes closing as she enjoyed every dark, delicious morsel. "Good choice, honey," she told me. She smiled, blue eyes warm, her hair a new color this month, with hints of red in her short bob. Mom looked amazing for sixty-four, and I hoped I'd inherited her aging-gracefully gene as well as her sweet tooth.

Part of it, I knew, had to do with the fact that Mom never slowed down. She and her girlfriends had a competition going about who could outdo the other on their Fitbits. Mom, the natural competitor, always won, even if that meant doing laps around her kitchen at night.

Mom swallowed her bite of chocolate cake. "Oh, I forgot to ask. How was Dana's wedding?"

"Actually, it was more fun than I thought it would be," I said. And that had everything to do with one Robert Zappia. Just the memory of his intelligent, teasing eyes made me feel a little bit warmer, like someone had just added a log to the fireplace nearby. "Nice ceremony, fun crowd." Fun *person,* in particular. "And good cake."

Now was usually the time Mom asked me about the cake—how many layers and whether or not there was filling—because cake was always the thing Mom most wanted to know about. Most moms want to know about the wedding dress first, but not my mom. She had her priorities straight.

"Did Peter have fun?" Mom threw me for a loop. Because I hadn't been thinking about Peter at all. I was thinking about Robert—had been all morning, actually.

Nadia cleared her throat, hoping to signal to Mom it was a touchy subject, but Mom failed to take the hint. She stared at me, waiting for my answer.

"Peter didn't go," I admitted.

"He doesn't *do* weddings," Nadia piped in, and I glared at her. Mom didn't need to know that about Peter. Nadia glared right back at me.

"What do you mean, 'He doesn't do weddings?' What does that even *mean*?" Mom reached for another bite of cake. "Doesn't he plan to attend his *own* wedding?"

Oh, great. Here we go. The exact topic of conversation I wanted to avoid.

Nadia raised her eyebrows, her eyes never leaving mine. "*Good* question, Mom. Tell us about that, Cass."

She beamed at me, triumphant, and I let out a long breath and inwardly counted to ten so I didn't steal my sister's cheesecake (her second piece!) out of revenge.

"You know… Ah…" How to explain the

phenomenon—or lack thereof—of no-labels-Peter to my mom? "I don't think the marriage thing is really"—absolutely ever, in a million years—"in the cards for us."

I shrugged at Mom, hoping against hope this would be the end of it. After all, Nadia so nicely took the pressure off me to have grandkids, not that Mom hadn't dropped a hint or two that she'd like me to consider a family sometime soon.

Mom looked puzzled as she slowly put down her fork.

"Huh," she mused aloud. "You've been seeing each other for two years. You should know if he's the one, or at least potentially…"

Yes, but that was actually the beauty of Peter. He allowed me to avoid thinking about The One. I didn't have to worry about whether he measured up to Dad, whether I'd ever have what my parents did. This way, I could cruise along with Peter and be comfortable in my avoidance zone.

Mom read my face like a postcard. She grew alarmed and put her hand over her heart.

"Do you even *want* to get married?" Mom's fear sat plainly on her face. I knew why: her marriage to my dad was one of the greatest achievements of her life. I mean, yes, she had a tidy career as a realtor, and she was very proud of being a mom to us, but when she talked about Dad, even now, her face glowed with a certain kind of joy. I knew she wanted that for me.

I couldn't tell her I'd spent most of my adult life avoiding the whole idea of marriage and whether I could ever be as happy as my parents had been.

"Of course I want to get married," I reassured Mom, patting her hand. She let out a little sigh of relief, and the fear dissolved.

Nadia dropped her fork on her now clean plate. "You know, I was watching something about this very thing on TV the other day and I realize what your problem is…"

Uh…excuse me? "I didn't know I had a problem." *Going out with Peter is my choice,* I wanted to shout. *He's comfortable, and he doesn't pressure me, and he does his thing, and I do mine. It's kind of perfect.*

"Exactly." Nadia's face brightened. "The first step is admitting you have a problem."

I frowned at her. "But I'd have to know what my problem is before I can fix that problem." Right now, my problem might be a big sister who was butting in where her opinion wasn't wanted. I glared at her, and she glared back.

"Okay!" Mom cried, breaking up the tension. "You guys are talking in circles. Nadia, please explain."

"Cass," Nadia said, straightening a bit in her seat like she did before every big sister lecture. "You tend to go after the same kind of guy. You pick someone you think you can change or mold into what you want, but you can't, because it's not the man. It's you."

This all sounded far too familiar. "Wait a minute," I said. "I saw that. You're quoting…Dr. Susie?"

Nadia nodded, her enthusiasm not waning. "I am, and she's right. You have a history of picking the noncommittal guys. The kind of guys who never have any intention of committing long-term."

What's wrong with that? I wanted to ask. Besides, they weren't *all* noncommittal, raging jerk-faces.

"Don't get me wrong," Nadia continued. "They're all nice guys—Peter, Jamie, Jack…"

"What about Scott? Scott from college. He was…" Sweet, loyal. He always talked about a big house and white picket fence in the suburbs. About getting married and having kids… Then, I remembered he wasn't so loyal after all. He'd cheated on me with one of my sorority sisters. Hmm. Okay, bad example. I looked up to see Mom and Nadia exchanging knowing glances, clearly remembering that awful spring break.

"Oh…you're right. I do pick the wrong guys," I admitted now, realizing that as I flipped back through all my ex-boyfriends, they were all…actually… Well, more or less, jerk-faces. None of them had been truly serious about me or the future. "How did I not realize that until right now?"

I didn't know what was worse: that I might have terrible taste in men or that Nadia actually *had* been right about me and might tell me *I told you so* for the rest of my life. She smiled at me now, though, her expression soft.

"Because you're competitive," she said in a loving way that made me instantly forgive her. I knew she just wanted to look out for me. "You like a challenge."

"Peter is a great guy." I didn't sound very convincing to my own ears.

"And very easy on the eyes," Nadia said, implying that I might have picked him only for his looks. Had I? When I thought about Peter's good qualities, why did I keep thinking of that strong chin and those stark blue eyes? "And you have nothing in common, and—"

We did have things in common. We… Well, we both liked chicken wings.

Uh-oh. Was that it? That and the fact that we both liked how Peter looked? He spent enough grooming time in front of the mirror for me to know he spent ample time admiring himself.

"He wouldn't even go to a wedding with you," Mom said.

"He hasn't even met Mom yet."

"He hasn't even *met me*," Mom reiterated. I glanced at her, sheepish. Right. He hadn't. He didn't want to meet Mom, but…part of me didn't want him to meet

Mom, either. I hadn't exactly been pushing for the two to get together. Why was that? Because I knew Mom wouldn't approve, that's why. Just like Nadia didn't approve.

"You're saying he's never going to commit?" I asked them both. "Are you saying…I should break up with him?"

Both Nadia and Mom squirmed in their chairs. They totally wanted me to dump him, but neither would say it out loud.

"What we're saying, dear," Mom began, "is that we want you to be happy." The way she looked at me now implied she thought I wasn't happy. But I liked my uncomplicated, not-labeled life with Peter. Didn't I?

"And to be happy," Nadia said, "you have to change the kind of guy you date."

"Right." I sucked in a breath.

"That seems simple, right?" Mom asked Nadia, and the two of them nodded vigorously. Right, simple. Just like that.

I took a sip of my lukewarm coffee. Why did I think nothing about this so-called strategy would be simple?

Five

I THREW MYSELF INTO WORK ON Monday, hoping to avoid thinking about what Nadia and Mom had been trying to tell me, which was that I had horrible taste in men and was single-handedly sabotaging any chance I had at happiness. The harder I tried *not* to think about it, the more I thought about it. I'd always figured that going for the fun guys, the no-label guys, made *me* fun and spontaneous. I prided myself on not being one of those plan-everything women, the ones who dated strategically only to snag a husband and obsessively clip bridal magazines (ahem, like Nadia at twenty-five). I wanted to have fun, to enjoy life, because, after all, a single car crash could change everything—like it had for my dad.

Anyway, all married people wanted to spawn more married people. I had a suspicion that married people were largely miserable and wanted *everyone* to be the same. Look at Michael and Nadia. The last time they'd been on a serious romantic date was... Well, nearly a year ago on their anniversary when I babysat for them. Still, the fact that *both* Mom and Nadia agreed I might be messing up my life gave me pause. Was I?

I wondered about this, even as I remembered Robert, the only other grown-up at Table Five. He'd said everyone wanted a happily-ever-aaaaaaah-fter. Did I? That was the million-dollar question. Did I want the happily-ever-after? It seemed like I was fighting it. Hard.

Soon, I'd have no time at all to think about this because I got a frantic email from one of my staff. An order for one of our most loyal clients, Peak Insurance, failed to arrive as scheduled. Worse, the owner of the company, George Kazminski, called to tell us he'd be stopping by the office to figure out what had happened. I'd barely gotten through the email when Phil, the new guy, a just-out-of-college hire that had started last week, burst into my office.

"George is here," he declared, a little out of breath.

"Where?" I asked, poking my head around the doorframe.

"I...I told him to wait outside."

I glared at Phil. "Outside the office?"

"I panicked," he admitted. I inwardly smacked my forehead.

"Go get him and bring him in," I admonished. If his dad hadn't been one of my most important clients when I was just starting out, I might never have hired Phil. His dad owned one of the largest grocery chains in the area, and he'd made *me* the single supplier of all their grocery bags, both disposable and recyclable. That account had launched my business.

I met George outside my office with a quick handshake and an apology. "I am so very sorry about this, George," I said, my face flaming with embarrassment as I felt my blood pressure rise. I hated disappointing clients, and George was as steady and loyal as they came. He wore one of his trademark three-piece suits. I'd never seen the man *not* wear a vest. Thankfully, his blue eyes showed no hint of anger.

"Don't worry, Cassandra," he said, shaking my hand warmly. "You and your staff have always come through for me."

"Just give me a second to find out what happened to your order."

Dana had put it in weeks before she'd left on her honeymoon. Or at least, I thought she had. What if all her dreaming about getting married had somehow distracted her from her job?

I scrubbed the unkind thought from my mind. Dana wouldn't let her work responsibilities slide, wedding or no. Since I hadn't been able to find the confirmation email in my inbox, I went to Dana's desk and began searching for a paper receipt. George stood nearby, admiring the view out the glass wall of the offices, the majestic Rocky Mountains behind us.

Hurriedly, I pawed through Dana's messy desk. Honestly, how could she find anything in there? I hoped I could block the cubical disaster from George. The last thing he needed was to see how things really were done around here—sometimes by the seat of our pants. I quickly searched, trying not to be distracted by the gleaming picture of her new groom, Jim Schmointz, staring out of a large 8x10 frame. I pulled open a drawer only to see two old copies of *Bridal Magazine* and a hard copy of *The Dater's Handbook* by Dr. Susie.

What? Did Dana believe in this, too? Maybe Dr. Susie helped her find the man of her dreams. Maybe Dr. Susie could take the credit for their blissful happiness. I shelved the thought for the time being so I could focus on finding the lost invoice.

"I remember we placed the order," I told George as I tried to make sense of Dana's lack of a filing system. "It was a thousand umbrellas and a thousand stress balls, all with your logo."

Just when I was about to give up, I found the file tucked beneath the latest edition of *Blushing Bride* magazine. I held up the folder, triumphant, and swung around in Dana's swivel chair.

"Well, you know how stressed-out insurance adjusters get," George said.

"And, apparently, you get wet, too," I murmured as I pored over the receipts. Dana put through the orders, so *where* were the products?

"That's funny," George said as he watched me, though he didn't laugh at my joke, treating me instead like a specimen under a microscope. "No, the umbrellas symbolize the coverage..."

"I don't know why the order didn't arrive at your office yet," I said, still studying the invoice in problem-solving mode. "It said it shipped. How about this? I'll double-check with the manufacturer, and I promise I will make this up to you."

"I know you will, Cassandra. You've always done a great job, and I have complete confidence in your company." He tucked his hands into his pockets and smiled at me, an earnest smile, almost too earnest. George always seemed so very serious, but then again, what else would someone expect from the president and owner of an insurance company?

"Thank you very much," I said, suddenly grateful that he was being so understanding. "That really means a lot to me."

George's gaze lingered a bit longer on mine, but then he nodded as he headed out.

"I'll take care of this," I called after him. He turned

and looked at me over his shoulder, as if he knew I would. I exhaled a sigh of relief as I watched George head out the door.

I glanced down at Dana's open office drawer, Dr. Susie's book, *The Dater's Handbook*, staring up at me. Curiosity won and I picked up the hardcover, randomly flipping it open.

"When you are together, you should be the only person he is focused on," I read aloud to Dana's empty cubicle. "You've agreed to spend your valuable time with him. You deserve his full attention. No distractions."

Huh.

I shut the book, hard. That seemed like obvious advice, didn't it? I mean, wouldn't everybody agree that you don't get together to ignore one another?

Just then, I got a text from Peter.

Wanna get together tonight?

Well, then. Why not test out the first bit of advice from Dr. Susie on Peter? He'd pass with flying colors, and then I could tell Nadia and Mom they were wrong. I wasn't single-handedly sabotaging my love life.

Peter asked me to meet him at the batting cages, which I figured meant he didn't want to wait around at his place for me to get off work. Despite not having played for the Rockies in two years, he still loved baseball. A knee injury had sidelined him from the game permanently, but not from practice, and he enjoyed swinging the bat most afternoons. When I arrived, I expected him to stop batting and maybe go change for dinner. I figured the "getting together" part included dinner.

I'd figured wrong.

Peter kept hitting ball after ball, in no hurry to change out of his sweats, Rockies shirt, and batting helmet. He cracked another ball into the netting.

"When you said we'd have plans tonight," I began as tactfully as I could as I sat on a bench behind the protective net, legs crossed and wearing a brand-new pair of heels, "I don't know…I thought we'd be doing something together."

"We are together," Peter said, keeping his eye on the automatic pitching machine. "We're at the batting cages."

He hit another ball with a crack that sounded as loud as a gunshot and made me flinch.

"Booyah! Did you see that?" He turned to me, excited, a boyish grin on his face.

"Uh…yeah, I did see that." I cleared my throat and glanced down at my new sleek pumps. Had they been a wasted purchase? "I don't know if this batting cage thing is really my idea of being together."

"Why? We are…" But he focused on the ball that had just been spit out from the machine. He swung his bat and connected, hard. I realized he'd barely even looked in my direction since I'd sat down, and his focus was entirely on the incoming baseballs. "We're totally together."

"Okay, if by 'together' you mean I'm on this side of the fence and you're on that side…" *And, by the way, not paying me any attention. At all.*

Peter turned, frowning slightly and appearing a bit annoyed. "Okay, well, what do you want to do?"

"I don't know. I thought maybe we could go somewhere, face each other. Talk. Maybe have dinner?"

He'd already turned away from me and was getting ready to connect with another ball. He smacked it and shook his head. "Wow," he murmured, clearly enamored with the bat. "Why can't I connect like this all the time?"

I realized he'd only been half listening to me—the farthest thing from forming a meaningful connection.

"Peter! I need you to focus."

But Peter kept his attention on the ball machine. "You need…" He hit another ball. "What?"

He readied for the next pitch.

"Peter!" I shouted, growing annoyed. He turned then, missed the pitch, and let out a groan. He glanced at me.

"What is going on?" he asked, frowning slightly.

How many times had I sat right here in these very batting cages? How many times had I waited for Peter to…engage…to do something? To really *see* me. To really *listen* to what I was saying. More times than I could remember.

"I'm on this side and you're on that side and we're not together, and I don't just mean tonight." My words spurted out in a rush. "We're at the restaurant and I'm with Nadia and Michael, and we go to a party and it's like you forget that I'm even there, or I go to a wedding of one of my closest friends, and you don't even come with me, you know? What's going on?"

And I meant that in a bigger sense—not just about our lack of real dates, but what's going on with…*us*. What *was* this? A relationship? I was dangerously close to asking him to put a label on it because without a label, I realized I had no idea why I should be with Peter.

"I don't know, Cass." Peter shook his head. My questions made him think, and he didn't like to think. Didn't I know that? He liked things simple and uncomplicated. He liked *not* to label anything for this reason. He didn't have to think about it and he didn't have to feel. "I'm not really sure what you want me to say."

I want you to tell me you love me, that I'm your

girlfriend, that we could be something more… I want you to tell me that you're in this with me, this relationship… this life!

It hit me like a fastball then. I'd never hear those words from Peter. He wasn't into anything but himself. He didn't want a real partnership—or frankly, a real anything—except finding a new sauce for chicken wings.

I sighed then, because I knew it was over. I'd been avoiding this conversation for two years because in my heart of hearts, I'd always suspected that we weren't good together.

"Nothing," I told Peter, tears springing to my eyes as I realized this—whatever it was—had just died. Nothing could bring it back to life. "I don't want you to say anything."

Peter turned his back on me, not much caring I was upset. But then again, when did he ever care about my feelings? I sniffed, fighting back a tear and stood, grabbing my bag. I heard the crack of his bat as he exclaimed, "See ya! That one had a flight attendant on it. Did you see that?"

But I'd already made it to the door, and I didn't look back. We were done.

Six

PETER TRIED A FEW HALF-HEARTED texts and one phone call to reach out to me over the next couple of weeks, but to no one's surprise, he didn't pursue me that hard. I couldn't believe a two-year relationship—if that's what you could call it—could unwind so quickly and so quietly. We had no big blow-out fight, no drama. I realized I'd been sleepwalking through the last two years, content with skating through life with a sort-of, part-time boyfriend, happy *not* to have to fend off all the questions about when I was going to find someone.

When I told Mom and Nadia the news—via text—I was eternally grateful neither one of them acted too happy about it. It wasn't like they were ever real Peter fans. Nadia offered to take me out to dinner to cheer me up—just us two—and I gratefully went.

I knew, on some level, I'd never really loved Peter.

What *did* we have in common? Nadia had been right about that. But, I felt sad. Not because I'd lost Peter, but because, I realized, I'd never really had him in the first place. Maybe part of me had hoped he would come around, or that he'd change, or that he'd challenge me to take our relationship to the next level. I'd been hanging around wishing that he'd turn into a different person.

Nadia met me at the restaurant. I managed to get through the whole meal without fielding any awkward, post-break-up questions about Peter. Nadia seemed to sense I didn't want to talk about it, that I'd rather hear about Jeremy and Michael, and be distracted with stories that had nothing to do with my love life. After dinner, she suggested we go see a movie. We took a cab to the closest theatre, since parking downtown could be a bit of a bear. Rain trickled down on the wet pavement, matching my mood.

She asked about Peter just as we arrived and I paid the cab driver, who let us out down the block from the movie theatre.

"You know what? You were right. Things weren't going well with Peter and he didn't seem to care if they did."

"Same old, same old." Nadia glanced at me. "So… good for you. You okay?"

"Yeah," I said, being honest. "I mean, I think part

of me knew he was never going to be The One." Or heck, even in the same solar system as The One.

A theatre poster showing a woman in a low-cut dress caught Nadia's attention. She stopped and rubbed her pregnant belly that grew larger every day. "Seriously? What makes them think anyone could wear that? And she's clearly not six months pregnant."

"You're tilting at windmills again," I told her. She'd gotten this way during her last pregnancy, but the railing against the patriarchy seemed a little bit worse this time around.

"They mock me," she said and I patted her arm sympathetically. "Real women are not built like that. Well…" She glared at me and my form-fitting jacket and jeans. "You are, but you're a freak."

"Stop," I admonished her, even though I knew she wouldn't.

As if Nadia weren't gorgeous in her own right. She was only a smidgen taller than me, and one dress size bigger. That single dress size difference had somehow meant a lifetime of me being the skinny sister.

Nadia tucked an arm under mine as a way of an apology. She pulled me closer as we walked down the sidewalk.

"Maybe it's time to try something new and break the habit of always choosing the wrong guy, time after time."

Great, we were back on Peter and how I was sabotaging my love life. Maybe I should steer her closer to that swimsuit ad at the bus stop nearby and distract her once more. "Maybe seek some professional help…"

"What?" Was she saying I needed counseling?

"In the form of, say…a manual. Or a handbook of some sort."

"You're saying I should consult *The Dater's Handbook*. I get it," I said, proud of myself for containing my skeptical eye roll to my imagination.

"How could it hurt?" Nadia seemed really committed to this idea.

"Funny, I saw a copy of it in Dana's desk." That book did seem to pop up all the time in my life. Was the universe trying to tell me something?

"As in Dana who just married the Schmointz of her dreams? Try the book. Worst case—you end up where you are now. Best case—you meet your own Schmointz, fall in love, and live happily ever after."

There that happily-ever-after thing was again.

"I don't know." I hesitated. The fastest way to get Nadia off this crazy idea was to agree with her, and yet, I couldn't quite get myself to do it. "It seems so desperate."

"Cass, Dr. Susie is a love and relationship expert. She has seven published books, all of them bestsellers."

63

"I know." Now I couldn't even contain the eye roll.

"She lectures all over the country."

"Mmm-hmmm." Okay, if this went on for much longer, I was going to steer her over to the bikini ad.

"In fact, she's giving a talk on *The Dater's Handbook.* Tonight. "

Nadia stopped walking and nodded to the sign behind me. I saw Dr. Susie's overconfident face staring back at me from the poster outside the small theatre. I'd been set up! Nadia dragged me here on purpose. She used the move as a ruse. I glared at her.

"I'm as shocked as you are," she lied badly.

"Uh-huh. Sure." I crossed my arms and then saw my salvation: the "sold-out" sign on the marquee. I pointed at it, but when I turned back to Nadia, she held up two tickets. Of course. She'd probably had this planned out for weeks.

I followed Nadia inside, and we took our seats.

"I'm going to get you back for this," I told Nadia, figuring the *next* time she needed emergency babysitting, I'd just have to be busy.

"I'm doing this for your own good," Nadia whispered.

The lights dimmed, and Dr. Susie walked onstage to roaring applause from the mostly rabid audience. *Whoa.* I glanced around at the women who'd mostly jumped to their feet in excitement as they clapped, and saw they weren't the weird, desperate types I'd imagined. They all looked...mostly normal. Professional, like me. All in their late twenties to late thirties, all seemingly put together and most of them decent-looking. *Why couldn't these women find good men?*

Then I remembered Peter. Maybe the question wasn't that they couldn't find good men. Maybe they couldn't find *better* men. I considered this as I listened to Dr. Susie, who wore a black and white suit with her blonde hair up in a French twist and her makeup, as usual, flawless.

I had to admit the woman made a good case for being an expert. She had the audience eating out of her hand in a matter of minutes. Even I found myself leaning forward a bit, paying closer attention than I thought I would during the forty-five minute lecture on why we're all preventing ourselves from being successful in love. Dr. Susie believed we're all, in some way or another, settling. The whole key to the HEA, as she called the happily-ever-after, revolved around saying *no* more often than we said *yes* to men who failed to meet our needs.

It made me wonder. Had I said *no* enough? Had I really screened guys, other than by looks or whether they made me laugh? Dr. Susie told the audience in no uncertain terms that we ought to have several absolute "deal-breakers" for men, and we'd need to stick to our guns.

What *were* my deal-breakers? Frankly, in that moment, I couldn't say.

I'd never admit this to Nadia, but the lecture got me thinking about my personal life in a way I hadn't in a long time. When Dr. Susie announced she'd be selling and signing copies of her new book, nearly the whole auditorium lined up for a copy. This was clearly how she made her money, I figured. That, and the cost of the ticket, which wasn't all that cheap as I stared at my stub.

"Let's go get in line," Nadia said, hustling me over to a group of people by a table piled high with copies of *The Dater's Handbook.*

"No. That's okay, really, I…" Dr. Susie had given me a lot to think about, but that didn't mean I was one hundred percent ready to jump on *The Dater's Handbook* bandwagon. Nadia, however, grabbed two copies of the book from the table and pulled me into line. It seemed to take forever for us to make it to the front, and I was beginning to wonder if Dr. Susie might get a hand cramp from all those signatures. When it was our turn, finally, I heard Dr. Susie plug her audio book as we stepped up to the table. Nadia nudged me forward.

"I'm your sister and I support you," Nadia said,

and before I could say another word, I felt Dr. Susie's attention on us.

"Hi. I'm married," Nadia blurted.

Great. Some support. She'd basically just said, "You don't need to Doctor-Susie me," and threw up her hands.

"Congratulations," Dr. Susie told Nadia. "Hopefully, you will read my book and it will validate your choice in husband."

"Make it out to 'Nadia,'" she said, handing Dr. Susie the book. Nadia glanced at me. I stared back, hoping she wasn't going to do what I thought she was going to do. "This is my sister, Cass."

"Hi." I waved, a little begrudgingly.

"It's not the man, it's *her*. It *really* is," Nadia said, making me sound like I was dating disabled. "That's why we're here."

"Thank you." I glared at Nadia, crossing my hands across my chest. "I feel really great about myself right now."

"Oh, no. Don't be embarrassed," Dr. Susie reassured me, her warm blue eyes ticking back and forth between me and my sister. "You're not alone in this. And, honestly, I wouldn't have written this best-selling book or be giving these sold-out lectures if it wasn't for the fact that I was just like you once, facing the same obstacles."

I felt a little better, anyway. Dr. Susie was nicer than I'd thought she'd be. I mean, she did plug her book right there *again,* but maybe she did have some good advice.

"She goes for the noncommittal guys," my sister said.

Seriously, Nadia? Are we airing all *my dirty laundry right here?*

"It's not that they're *all* noncommittal," I protested. Then I thought about it for a second. "It's just they all seem to have a history of..." Being self-involved? Putting their needs before mine? Not being, in any way, serious about a relationship? Ugh. Now, I'd painted myself in a corner. "Not actually committing," I finished, lamely.

"I see." Dr. Susie studied me, and her sharp eyes seemed to bore right into me. "If you're picking the noncommittal guys, maybe *you're* noncommittal."

And, just like that, I felt the truth in that statement. Wasn't that why I'd stayed with Peter so long? Because I didn't really want to think about The One or happily-ever-afters...or letting myself hope that there could actually *really be* an "ever after"?

"Ooooh, I never thought of that," piped in Nadia, a light bulb going off for her, too. "Oh, you're good."

Too good, maybe. Nadia would no doubt be harping on my commitment phobia from here on out.

"The truth is, nobody wants to admit they want the predictable, consistent, same-routine-every-day kinda guy," Dr. Susie said. "We all think we want the unpredictable, rebellious, exciting guys. But those are the ones who are never content. They need to keep moving, always looking for the next thing, and that means *you* will never be enough. That's why they can't commit."

Was that true? I thought about Peter, Jack, and Scott. They *were* all in some ways unpredictable, definitely independent, and maybe a little restless. Jack owned a motorcycle, after all. Maybe Dr. Susie was right.

"Wow," Nadia said, awe in her voice. "You are really good."

Nadia wasn't wrong. Everything she said seemed to make perfect sense.

"I know," Dr. Susie said, not at all embarrassed to boast about it. "Cass, my husband is consistent and predictable and average in every way. He brings home a steady paycheck; he always asks about my day. He doesn't look around constantly for the next thing when you're sitting right in front of him. Now, that is commitment."

She'd gotten me. She had. Because right then, in that moment, I realized that's exactly what I wanted: a real partner, someone to share my life with, not someone like Peter who flirted with every pretty girl to walk into his bar. Standing here in front of Dr. Susie, I knew, for the first time in my adult life, I was ready to get serious about finding The One.

And it started with *The Dater's Handbook.*

I grabbed one out of Nadia's hand. "Make it out to 'Cass,'" I said, holding the book out to Dr. Susie.

"Oh, Cass!" Nadia gave me a big hug, a huge smile on her face.

This, I vowed, would be a new beginning. No more noncommittal guys. Now, I'd be serious in my search for The One.

Seven

I RAN WITH DUKE DOWN THE trail Saturday morning, an overcast fall day with the wind whistling through the tall evergreens. Because I'd vowed to turn over a new dating leaf, instead of the usual REO Speedwagon blaring on my iPod, I'd put on the audio edition of *The Dater's Handbook* and had been diligently listening to Dr. Susie. Granted, it was getting harder and harder to upload things to my old iPod, and I'd held on to it longer than I should have, but it had been a high school graduation present from Dad. When I held it, I thought of him. He'd probably be all for me choosing better guys. He'd always told me I deserved the best, and I knew I hadn't been picking the best for myself.

"Welcome to *The Dater's Handbook.* If you are listening to this audio recording, that means you've made the conscious decisions to improve your love life and change the way you look at the opposite sex," Dr. Susie declared in a tone brimming with confidence. It was hard not to believe she did have all the answers.

"I will show you why the men you're choosing are the wrong men, and I will help you break that pattern to find Mr. Right and get the happily-ever-after that you deserve," she continued. There it was again: the HEA. That's what I wanted, wasn't it? I remembered my parents, heads together at the kitchen sink, giggling over some inside joke, maybe when I was in fourth grade. That was what love looked like to me: two people, madly in love despite being married fifteen years, still able to make each other laugh. Yes, that was what I wanted.

I thought again about Robert from Dana's wedding reception—his dark, intelligent eyes, the way he matched me joke for corny joke—and wondered why my thoughts had wandered back to him. He'd been handsome, sure, but what I'd really liked was how he'd made me laugh that night. A lot. Not that I'd ever see him again, though. I'd bolted from that wedding in my haste to stay loyal to Peter. Ugh. When I thought about how that no-labeled relationship had worked out... I should've stayed at the wedding.

With the Rocky Mountains at our back, I decided to take a detour to let my golden retriever get a little more time off-leash at the local baseball park, now empty since late fall had turned too cold for games. We'd probably only get a week or two before the snow began to fall in earnest. I freed Duke from his leash and let him run. He galloped across the park, tail wagging and tongue out, happy and content.

We weren't the only ones trying to take advantage of the time before the snow. On the far end of the park, I saw another dog, a retriever mutt, maybe, and his owner. I plucked out my earbuds, pausing Dr. Susic. I locked eyes with the owner.

A thrill of recognition surged through me.

Robert.

I froze as a buzz of excitement tickled the back of my neck. It was as if, just by thinking of him, I'd conjured Robert up in person. I'd snuck out of the wedding afraid to catch a bouquet and now, here we were, face to face. Should I say hi? Or turn and run the other way to avoid an awkward explanation of why I'd ducked out of the reception without a good-bye?

Duke made that decision for me as he rushed to the chain link fence behind home plate at right about the same time Robert let loose his dog's ball, which sailed high and landed with a *plink* against the chain link right by my face.

Robert glanced up and saw me then, a sheepish look crossing his features. "Hey," he called. "Sorry about that." He trotted over and grasped the fence between us. He was more handsome than I remembered, his longish hair poking out of his wool cap, his light blue jacket nearly matching mine. We looked like we'd coordinated outfits.

"Were you *trying* to hit us with your ball?" I teased, as I grabbed Duke by the collar in case he decided that ball was *his.*

"No," Robert said, a slow, sly grin spreading across his face. "This is for protection. You might be carrying a concealed cake fork."

I laughed, recalling how I'd stolen a bite of his cake at the reception. Touché. He moved around the fence barrier, closer to me. He was tall and fit, more so than I remembered, but those intelligent, dark eyes were the same. They never left mine.

"Hi," he said.

"Hi," I answered, feeling suddenly a little shy.

"Who's this?" He bent down to scratch Duke behind the ears.

"This is…uh, Duke." I let Duke go. He happily jumped around Robert's legs, tail wagging fiercely. Duke liked him, a lot. "And who's that?" I nodded at the dog standing behind him.

"This is Daisy." No sooner were the words out of his mouth, the dog took off running. Duke trotted off after her, happy to participate in an impromptu game of chase.

"I just got her last week from the shelter," Robert said, watching Duke and Daisy trot across the outfield. He'd adopted a shelter dog? My heart was melting. Men who love animals? They're my soft spot.

"Can you believe someone left her on the side of the road?"

"No." I shook my head. I hated hearing stories of animal cruelty. Who could treat an animal that way? Duke trusted me more than anything, and I couldn't imagine violating that trust.

"Apparently, she's a very good retriever," he said, and he tossed the ball hard. Both dogs ran after it across right field. "So, um…" He cocked his head to one side. "Do you come here often?"

"Is that an actual question, or…is that an incredibly cheesy, and *dated*, pick-up line?"

"Both." Robert's grin grew bigger, his brown eyes warmer.

"Yes," I admitted. "We come here a couple of times a week." It made me wonder if Robert lived nearby. He must have, right? The dogs came back, both tugging on the oversized rubber ball, neither one wanting to give it up.

"I'm sorry I didn't get to say good-bye to you at the wedding." *He* was sorry? I was the one who'd snuck out.

"Oh, no, that's okay." A sting of guilt pricked me.

How could he say good-bye when I'd practically bolted for the door?

"I wanted to…uh…" He paused, and I remembered exactly what he'd wanted to do—ask me out. I'd overheard him tell the flower girl he'd planned on it. I felt a tingle in my toes. Was he going to ask me now? What would I say? With Peter out of the way, I no longer had an obstacle to saying yes. Did I? Confusion whirled in my brain. I'd only just started to listen to Dr. Susie, and while my gut told me I wanted to get to know Robert better, I'd recently learned my instincts were terrible. For example, see: Peter. Jack. Scott… Pretty much every man I'd ever dated.

Robert's phone rang.

"I think that's your cue?" I wondered if this was fate intervening.

"Don't go," he said and reluctantly pulled his phone from his pocket. "No, wait, I have to take this, but…" He answered the call and I moved away.

"Good to see you!" I called, as I headed to Duke. I latched his leash to his collar as Robert reached out, as if to stop me.

"Let me call you right back," he told whoever was on the other line.

"Duke!" he shouted. "Before she disappears again, would you ask your mother if she'd like to go on a date with me?"

I giggled a little. Maybe he *was* serious about seeing me again. And apparently, he'd also figured out I'd left that wedding reception quickly on purpose. "Okay, Mr. Zappia," I said. "I *will* go out on a date with you."

"Good. Now, what's your phone number? It might be hard to make plans if I have to stalk you at random parks."

I laughed again as we exchanged numbers.

The following Monday, I was met with another work disaster. Phil, the new guy, had struck again, but this time, by messing up an order of small, souvenir Tornadoes soccer league balls. Today was the day Dana returned from her honeymoon, thank goodness. In the meantime, I had to break the news to Phil that he'd screwed up—again.

"We have a slight problem with the Tornadoes order," I told him and tossed him a small black and blue football with the Tornadoes logo on it. "The order was for a thousand *fútbols*."

Phil glanced at me, blankly, *still* not getting it. "Okay...and..."

"And these are for a soccer giveaway for their game in Argentina. You know, where they play *fútbol*." I literally mimed kicking a soccer ball. Now, Phil finally got it.

He laughed. As if this was a laughing matter! The company would eat the cost of these footballs. "Ah, honest mistake. *Fútbol.* Football." He shrugged. Did this kid not know this was serious business? I could *fire* him, and yet, he didn't even seem fazed.

"Uh, yeah." I stared at him. He looked at me, blankly.

"What do you want me to do?"

I took a deep breath. I needed to *train* him, I reminded myself, show him how he could fix problems. Heck, show him that *this was a problem*.

"First, let's get the correct balls manufactured. Second, I found a high school in Wichita, their colors are black and blue, their mascot is the tornado…"

Phil looked at me like I was speaking another language.

"Maybe you could *call* them and see if they'd be interested in the footballs. Maybe we could recover some of our losses?"

Phil frowned slightly. "That seems like a lot of work."

A lot of *work*? He'd lost my company thousands of dollars!

"Yes, Phil. It is." I glared at him a beat, hoping that he got the message.

He seemed to finally understand. "Oh, uh, got it. Okay."

"Cass!" Dana arrived just then, and I'd never been so glad to see her. My most competent worker back from her honeymoon.

"Hey." I wrapped her in a tight hug. She seemed tanned and happy, oversized sunglasses on her head, even though, outside, a bank of clouds covered the sky. "Don't you look all relaxed! Welcome back."

"It's good to be back," she said and grinned at me.

"Well, you're bursting at the seams, so tell me, how was it?"

"It was *ah-mazing*," she cooed. "A beachfront bungalow with our own private palapa. I love palapas!"

"Who doesn't?" I said, having no idea what a palapa even was. "I mean, even the name sounds fun. Palapa!"

"Palapa!" she echoed, excited. "I don't think there is anywhere more romantic than a palapa in Acapulco."

While I loved that Dana was happy, part of me just wasn't sure I was quite ready to hear all this. It was almost...too much. Was I jealous? Maybe. But, I was also trying to run a business, not that Phil understood that concept.

I clapped my hands, knowing if I didn't stop this talk of Acapulco, it would go on all morning.

"Well, back to reality. I need that JB contract, and can you schedule a meeting with Stan Morris? That would be great."

"Yes, okay." Dana didn't lose a single watt in her

smile. One of many reasons I loved her. She always took on assignments happily. I was about to head back to my office when she stopped me. "Oh! I just have to say something. At my wedding, you and Robert looked really great together and…"

I felt heat rise to my face. "He already asked me out," I admitted.

"Oh…yay!" Dana clapped her hands and stomped her feet and gave a little squeal of joy. I self-consciously swept my hair off my forehead. I was glad *she* was so excited. But then again, I was a little excited too, I had to admit. I thought about Robert's lopsided smile. His amazingly quick wit. How he kept me on my toes. Yes, I was absolutely looking forward to seeing him again.

Eight

THEN CAME THE AGE-OLD DILEMMA. What to
wear?

I tried and discarded a few outfits before
finally settling on a basic black tank top, torn jeans,
and of course, my new suede boots with the slender
heels. Robert was tall, and I should make the most of
that.

I felt butterflies flutter in my stomach, took a deep
breath, and glanced at my reflection in the mirror.
Ugh—I even *looked* nervous, my dark eyes a little too
wide, my smile a little too forced. It had been more
than two years since I'd been on a first date, after all.
Would I even remember how to do it? As the nerves
pricked my belly, I realized Peter had served another
very important purpose: keeping me from having to
endure the dreaded awkward first date.

A million thoughts bounced against each other

in my brain like bumper cars: would I kiss him? Did I want to kiss him? Would we get along as well as I remembered, or would it be an evening punctuated with odd silences? I did not like first dates, I realized. I hated the unknown of them, the billion ways they could go horribly wrong.

Before Peter, I'd had a string of bad first dates, including one where the guy downed three Old Fashioneds in the span of fifteen minutes. By the appetizers, he was too drunk to properly string a sentence together. Worse, the man "forgot" his wallet, so I'd been stuck with the whole check. Clearly, there'd been no date two. Of course, by the time Peter had come around, it had made *sense* to go for him. He'd not ordered three drinks in three minutes, he never forgot his wallet, and being with him meant that I could put off the whole first-date fiasco.

I can do this, I told the mirror silently. I knew I could. I needed to if I was going to get beyond the curse of my poor-decision-making past. I took a deep breath and tuned back into my iPod attached to the speakers on my bathroom counter. Dr. Susie's voice sounded calm and full of reason as she narrated Chapter One.

"The first date is the opportunity he has to show you what type of effort he's going to put into this relationship. Does he make plans and capture your personality? The first date should be fun, appropriate, and something you'd enjoy."

Right. I tried to remember the first time I'd gone out with Peter. I think it was to his own sports bar. Not exactly in keeping with my personality, since sports weren't my thing unless Boston College was playing. My doorbell rang, and I instantly jumped. *Ack!* He was here.

I smoothed down my hair one last time as I glanced at my reflection in the mirror and scurried over to my foyer. Duke barked once and wagged his tail as I swung open the door.

Robert stood there, dark hair perfect, grinning from ear to ear.

"Hey," he said, and I felt his perfectly pitched, low baritone reverberate in my stomach. I loved his voice, all warm and smooth, like drizzled chocolate over ice cream.

"Hey," I said back, my nerves vanishing. He wore jeans and a simple gray sweater, looking good but not trying too hard.

"You look...amazing." His eyes swept my casual outfit, lingering on my new suede boots. Good. I wore them to be noticed.

He stepped in, and for a heart-stopping second, I thought he might kiss me right here on my doorstep. Instead, he pulled me in for a hug. He was big and warm and strong, his arms feeling as if they belonged around me, and I inhaled the scent of his sweet and spicy aftershave. He backed away and held up a small bag of neatly tied doggie treats from the local bakery. "I got these for Duke, since I didn't want him to be lonely without you tonight."

Duke barked his appreciation and wagged his tail. "Smart man," I said.

"I try." He shrugged and handed me the treats. I took them and put them in Duke's bowl, where he began eating them eagerly. No flowers, then, but he *did* think of my dog, which was more important to me than something pretty to put in a vase. "So, where are we off to?"

"How's your golf game?" he asked me, the hint of a teasing smile on his face.

When he pulled into Joe's Putt-Putt Funland, I thought he was kidding at first. After all, Joe's Putt-Putt Funland came second only to Pizza Gameland as *the* place to go for every ten-year-old's birthday party. I realized with a start I hadn't been here since I'd come with Dad when I was a sophomore in high school, back when he was trying to convince me I wasn't "too grown-up" for a place like Funland. Dad had always thought too many adults spent too much time *not*

having fun when stuff like air hockey and video games could put a smile on anyone's face.

"We're going...here?" I glanced at Robert.

"What? You afraid I'm going to beat you?" He grinned as he got out of the car and hurried around to my side. He opened my door. "My lady," he said and bowed like a knight of old. I had to laugh as I hopped out and followed him inside.

Still, a nagging little voice of doubt popped up in my head. Dr. Susie'd said first dates should be *appropriate.* Was mini-golf appropriate for a first date with a grown woman and not a fourteen-year-old? Plus, I had flashbacks to Peter and the batting cages. Was this one of those times I'd just sit around and watch someone else have all the fun?

But as Robert gathered up our putters and our balls, I found myself getting just a little bit excited. I wasn't going to be sidelined this time. Dad had been right to drag me here as a surly teen. I'd had fun, despite myself.

"Ladies first," Robert said, bowing once more as I put my yellow golf ball down on Hole One. I stood slightly to the left. I knew this hole. If you stood right in the center, the giant robot T. Rex would come to life and startle you when you were about to swing. I gave my ball a good smack, banking it off the left wall. It came to a rest just inches from the hole.

"I think I'm being hustled," Robert said, staring at me with suspicion and the hint of a smile on his face.

"Your turn," I told him, a challenge in my voice.

"Watch and learn," Robert said as he put his ball down on the green right in the middle. The T. Rex predictably roared to life, making him jump and smack his ball hard right, away from the hole. I had to giggle. He'd fallen for the first trap.

"Don't worry," I tried to assure him. "He's an herbivore. He only eats trees and bushes and golf balls."

"That's not an herbivore," Robert declared. "That's a Tyrannosaurus Rex. I want a mulligan."

"Man up, friend," I said, laughing. "The obstacles are part of mini-golf."

I set up for my next shot, which I saw was about six inches to the hole. But just as I tapped the ball, Robert appeared and knocked it out of the way with his putter.

"Oh! That is *so* sad," he teased.

"That's *not* sad, that's called cheating."

Robert coughed. "You just told me obstacles were part of miniature golf." He raised both eyebrows, and I had to laugh.

"Fine. Fair enough," I said, determined not to let him win this round. Two could cheat. He positioned himself by his ball and swung his club, and as the ball rolled closer to me, I stopped it with the toe of my boot, just inches from the hole. Then I kicked it away.

"Oh, *come* on, that's a foul!" Robert cried. "That's clearly a foul."

"There are no fouls in miniature golf," I said, grinning. It was my turn, and I glanced down at my yellow ball, far in the corner of the green. "I'm going to pick up my ball and put it back where it *should* be." I plunked it down where it had been before Robert had slapped it out of the way. "And that's a gimme."

"Tell you what," Robert said, as he squatted down, leaning on his putter as he eyed the shot. "I'll make you a wager."

I sank to the ground too, so we were nearly eye level. I loved bets.

"You sink that putt, you choose where we go on our second date," he declared, dark eyes never leaving mine. "You miss it, I get to choose where we go on our second date."

I rested my chin on the handle of my putter. "You're assuming we're *having* a second date."

"Oh, I am, and we are," Robert said. Had to love that confidence. Who didn't love a man who wasn't afraid to go after what he wanted? "The *where* is the only question."

"Okay. You ready?" I covered my eyes.

"Oh...blindfolded!" Robert sounded impressed.

I knocked the ball wildly on purpose. It swung just left of the hole. Dr. Susie would be proud. Even though I hadn't gotten to her chapter on second dates yet, I was pretty sure she'd say Robert needed to do the planning. He had to prove his level of effort, right?

"Did you just miss that on purpose?" Robert asked, calling me out.

"I didn't want to bruise your ego," I said, "so I made it interesting."

"You want interesting, huh? Let's see that one more time." He took my yellow ball and put it on the green next to the hole.

"Oh, I've got an idea," I said. I laid down on the green as if it were a pool table, and used the handle of my club to tap the ball. Again, I missed.

He grinned at me. "Now, I know you're doing that on purpose," he said. "Say, what do you say to a real game of pool?"

Upstairs, in the massive game room of Joe's Putt-Putt Funland, the "Funland" part included a mini arcade with skeeball and all the latest shoot 'em up games, as well as a whole corner of pool tables and air hockey. We headed for the left corner, where we set up a quick match of solids and stripes. Robert let me go first, which was his mistake—I nearly cleared the table on the first go.

"I am *totally* being hustled," Robert joked, shaking his head. "What do you do? Hang out here on the weekends and take money from unsuspecting twelve-year-olds?"

"Something like that." I laughed. "So, what do you do for a living?" I asked Robert as I lay over the corner of the pool table, about to sink the eight ball in our second game of solids and stripes. Robert just shook his head at me.

"Don't scratch," he warned, but I already knew I'd win the instant the stick touched the cue ball. It plunked into the corner pocket with no resistance.

Robert looked amazed.

"I am being hustled," he said, whistling.

"You were saying?" I asked him, prompting him to answer my question.

"I don't even know what I was saying—not after that shot."

I laughed. Despite his protests, Robert was a good sport. Not all guys felt that way about losing. Take Peter, for instance. The one time I'd beaten him at pool, he'd insisted on playing three more games. He had to beat me before his ego was fully healed.

"So, what do I do? I oversee operations of and the financial budgets for the city's parks and recreation department." Robert sat on the edge of the pool table at the corner closest to me.

"That sounds very important," I said, leaning toward him. "What made you want to get into that?"

"The free T-shirts," Robert said, a perfectly serious expression on his face.

"Excuse me?" He'd lost me.

"Yeah. Whenever there's an event that involves one of our facilities, I get to attend for free and I get a free T-shirt. Yesss!" He pumped a fist in the air. I laughed a little. "How about you?" he asked me as he slid off the pool table. "How did you get into marketing?"

"After college, I started out in a big conglomerate marketing firm tasked with increasing advertising and finding new avenues for promotion." I thought back to those first days out of college in that hectic environment where I seemed to have all the responsibility but none of the credit. I'd confided in Dad about how I'd felt like a cog in the wheel, and he was the one who'd encouraged me to go out on my own.

"When I learned how things worked," I continued, "and saw how much these companies were making by simply slapping a logo on stuff, I realized instead of going through a middleman, I could be the middleman. Plus, I wanted to work for the best boss in the world. And it turns out, that's this guy." I pointed at myself in the cheesiest way possible. "Right here." It was exactly what Dad had always said about working for himself. He'd had his own painting company, and he'd loved being his own boss.

"Wow, humble, too," Robert teased. "But, you know, good for you. It takes guts to go out on your own and start your own business."

It did, didn't it? It was the one thing people didn't tell me too often. Sure, Peter had owned his own bar, but he was never in any real danger of financial ruin. He had years of major league baseball paychecks stocked away in mutual funds to cushion him if his business ever failed. Me? I was all on my own, no trust fund in sight.

The rest of the date sped by all too quickly. Turned out, there was no need for me to be nervous. I felt like I'd known Robert all my life. We laughed at the same jokes, and I could break out my corniest ones and he'd still crack a smile. It was almost like we shared a brain.

The end of the date came far too soon. Where had the night gone? After he'd parked in the visitor's space of my condo building, and we'd walked the short distance to my front door, a gentle snow—the first of the season—began to fall. My nerves drummed in my stomach again. Was he going to kiss me? Did I want that? Part of me definitely did, but was I ready? Was I even sure Dr. Susie would approve? My instincts told me I wanted to plunge headfirst into a relationship with Robert, but my gut had steered me wrong in the past. Could I really trust it?

Robert faced me on my stoop, the soft snow falling around us. "I need to ask you a very personal question," he said. "And I want you to think really, really hard before you answer, because I'd like the truth."

He'd become so serious in that moment I began to wonder what it was all about. Was he going to ask me if it was okay that he had a wife in Arizona?

"I know we just met, and you really don't know me, but I have to know…"

I literally held my breath, waiting. Robert moved towards me. *Oh.* He was going to kiss me. I knew it. I glanced at his full lips, the serious look on his face. Yep, a kiss was coming.

"Did you miss that putt on purpose?" A goofy smile spread across his face, and instantly, the tension evaporated. I laughed.

"And what if I did?"

"Then I get to choose where we have our second date."

He stepped even closer, and I craned my neck up to meet his gaze. He was so tall.

"That would mean we both win," I managed, now overcome by his body, so near mine. Snow began to lightly dust his jacket. Somewhere in the distance, someone had lit a fire in a wood-burning fireplace, sending the scent straight to my front door.

"Awww." Robert cocked his head. "That's just so…"

"Cheesy," I said, rolling my eyes. Where had that sentimental sap come from? Oh, goodness. Was I turning into mush over here?

Robert cleared his throat. "Totally cheesy," he added, his dark eyes never leaving mine. Something about the way he looked at me told me he didn't mind. I couldn't help but notice his lips, full and perfect, seeming to be asking to be kissed. I wondered what kind of kisser he'd be.

"I had a good time," I said. And I did. I wanted badly to know what his lips felt like. All it would take was for me to reach up onto my tiptoes and press my lips against his. Was he moving closer? His eyes never left mine—dark, large, determined. But… I thought of Dr. Susie again and how she suggested women *not* get involved physically before they were sure he was a man worth pursuing. How when we get too physical too fast, we lose our ability to honestly evaluate a mate. Normally, I'd go with my gut and kiss Robert, but Dr. Susie taught me to second-guess my instincts. So, instead, I moved ever so slightly and pecked Robert on the cheek. He stiffened a little in surprise. Clearly, a kiss on the cheek wasn't what he'd expected.

"Good night," I said, and he stared at me a beat, a smile playing at the corner of his mouth. He wasn't offended. *Interesting.*

"Good night," he said, nodding his head a bit. I slipped inside my condo foyer door and shut it behind me, heart beating wildly. How I'd wanted to kiss him! But, I had to give myself props for resisting the temptation. I was learning *not* to go with my instincts. Maybe I'd finally turned over a new leaf. Mom and Nadia would be so proud. Still, I stood at the window of the door and watched Robert tug up his collar against the whirling snowflakes as he walked from my porch.

And I suddenly wanted that second date to come sooner, rather than later.

Nine

THE NEXT DAY, I JOINED Mom at Nadia and Michael's house to help prep for the big school bake sale. As always, Nadia took her mom bake-off responsibilities to the extreme. Her cupcakes *and* frosting were all homemade, all organic, and prepared with all locally grown farm-to-table products. Just watching her trot around her beautiful granite kitchen island made my head spin.

"Okay, let's move it, people," Nadia demanded of us. "The preschool fundraiser starts at noon, and I have a hundred of these things to deliver."

Mom and I glanced at each other, and I picked up the subtle raise of Mom's eyebrow. Nadia had told us how many cupcakes we needed regularly for the last fifteen minutes. *Okay, Nadia. We get it. One hundred cupcakes!* I'd landed frosting duty. Mom got sprinkles. Nadia kept double-checking our work, as if we both weren't dessert experts. Seriously, you did not need to show either of us how to lay down sugar confections.

Normally, my family and I bonded over sweets, but today was most definitely different. For one, Nadia wasn't allowing any of us to taste the cupcakes, and that was pure torture. And, secondly, while Nadia always ran her kitchen with an iron fist, today she was…particularly ruthless. She'd had me redo four iced cupcakes already.

Michael, dutifully clad in his apron decorated with colorful coffee cups, took out piping hot double-chocolate goodness from the oven and laid them on cooling racks. Nadia gently tucked each final dessert—only the ones that met her high standards—into the bakery boxes. I hadn't necessarily planned on bringing up Robert today, but if I didn't say something soon, I feared Nadia would try to separate the sprinkles by color.

"So…I had a date last night," I told them, eager to share my first post-Dr. Susie experiment.

"That's great!" Nadia exclaimed, excited for me for a brief blip before the persona of the Dictator Chef returned. "But…talk while you work," she admonished. Man, she was taking this bake sale thing too seriously. I mean, worst case, we go buy a few at the supermarket. Not that I'd ever dare say that. Not to Nadia, who believed store-bought goods were a pre-packaged, processed train straight to cancer town.

"What's his name?" Mom asked, eyes lighting up. Well, at least I'd distract her from the cupcake assembly line.

"Robert." Even as his name left my lips, I felt a little giddy. It was a good name, Robert. Solid. I thought about how he made me laugh and realized I liked his name quite a lot.

"Where did you meet him?" My mom seemed so eager for the details she was beginning to neglect her sprinkle duties.

"Wait," Michael interrupted as he set a piping hot tray of cupcakes on the kitchen counter. "What about Peter?"

"Cass and Peter broke up," Nadia informed him, sounding annoyed, as if this wasn't the first time she'd mentioned it. Sometimes, Michael didn't always listen, especially when there might be a football game on.

"Seriously?" Michael asked, astounded. Also, I'd admit, he looked a little sad, probably because he wouldn't get free chicken wings at Peter's bar anymore. And, to be fair, I'd always suspected Michael had a little man crush on Peter and loved telling people he knew a former Rockies player.

"That is so old news, hon," Mom said, shaking her head. Poor Michael. I almost felt bad for him, because he looked a little crestfallen. "Your date?" Mom glanced at me now, clearly wanting to know more. Mom, ever the romantic, loved tales of first dates.

"I met him at Dana's wedding. He's handsome, fit, he works for the city, has a dog…" I gushed, unable to stop myself. Why not tell them he has a great sense of humor, was playful, and I loved the way we could instantly make an inside joke out of anything at all?

"I like him already," Mom said, clearly seeing my excitement. "Was there a connection? Any sparks?"

"There were definite sparks." I thought about how I'd been so tempted to kiss him on my doorstep. Oh, my, but there were sparks.

"Uh-uh-uh," Nadia tsked, as she shut a full box of freshly decorated cupcakes. "'Excitement, passion, and sparks are not important. Consistency and reliability is the key.' That's what we're looking for."

I frowned. Did she actually just quote Dr. Susie, word for word? Also, what was this *we* business? *We* weren't dating. I was.

"Wow. You've memorized the book." I shook my head. Nadia was really going to superior lengths to lecture me on my love life this time.

"Wait." Michael paused, standing near Nadia. "What book?"

"Cass has turned her love life over to Dr. Susie and *The Dater's Handbook,*" Nadia told him, sounding proud. *Oh, brother.* "I'm coaching her."

Uh, yeah. I hadn't actually said she could "coach" me. I was doing just fine on my own, thank you very—

"Would this Robert be *Handbook* approved?" Nadia focused on me with a laser-like intensity I was sure she only saved for special occasions, like potty training my nephew. "Was he 'attentive'? Was he 'genuinely interested in what you have to say, or is he just there'?"

And are you going to give me a chance to answer any of these questions? I wanted to ask but didn't.

"Yes, he paid complete attention to me, and it felt good." This was the truth. Robert's attention—and those amazing dark eyes—had been focused on me the entire night.

"Good. Robert passed the first test," Nadia said. Mom let out a little sigh. She clearly didn't believe in "tests" when it came to love. She was in the you're-in-love-or-you're-not camp. But Nadia wasn't finished. "Remember, one good date does not a relationship make."

Was Nadia speaking slowly for my benefit? Did she think I was hearing-impaired as well as relationship-impaired? Michael snuck behind her, grabbed a fully iced cupcake, and took a giant bite. I didn't even warn Nadia. She kind of had that one coming.

"You have to be sure to be open to other opportunities," Nadia continued in that nasally, lecturing tone of hers. Boy, did I hate it when she lectured. But I also knew her well enough to know arguing was pointless. I just had to let her make her point, or she'd press it for days.

"For sure," Michael agreed, mouth full as he put his hand on Nadia's shoulder. She noticed he'd stolen a cupcake.

"Seriously?" She let out a frustrated sigh. "Uh, sometimes it's like I already have two children."

"Three," Michael mumbled, pointing to me as I tasted a bit of frosting. I was caught. But, honestly, all the lecturing made me want to eat. Besides, my inner sweets monster had to be appeased, and the frosting smelled—and tasted—delicious.

"Uh," Nadia growled, not happy.

"Does this mean I'm off the cupcake assembly line?" I asked, hopeful.

"Not a chance," Nadia barked, pointing to a new pan I had to frost. Oh, well. It was worth a shot.

Nadia ended up rocking the bake sale. Her all-organic, non-GMO, farm-to-table cupcakes were a huge hit. I dove back into work Monday morning, even though most of my attention was focused on Robert. He'd texted a few times over the weekend—funny, little, no-pressure texts, like the picture he took of a man jogging in the park and dragging a tractor tire behind him. That and his caption, "Is this how they're mowing the park grass now?" made me laugh out loud. His regular but not overwhelming presence on my phone made me smile. Robert, himself, just instantly brought a smile to my face. Made me remember how fun being playful could be, how life wasn't all...serious. But then I thought about Dr. Susie and Peter. Peter hadn't been serious, either, had he? In fact, he was pretty much the poster child for a boy-man, someone intent on not growing up.

While I was pondering this *and* trying to locate an order that had disappeared from our system, George Kazminski popped into the office, taking me by surprise.

"Hi, Cassandra," he said, looking all adult in his crisp three-piece suit. For a second, my heart stopped. Had we messed up his order—again? *Tell me no!* "Are you busy?"

"George... Hi! No, I just wasn't expecting to see you here." *Please tell me those stress balls and umbrellas made it like they were supposed to.* I'd had Dana double-check, and I was sure they had, but still...

"I know and I'm sorry to drop by unannounced. I just wanted to thank you in person. You really went above and beyond the normal customer service on our order."

I let out the breath I'd been holding. *Oh, thank goodness.* Everything was okay. "You're welcome," I said, the tension leaving my shoulders. "And it was my pleasure. Your business is important to us." *Because it's so very regular and dependable. Just like all insurance carriers.*

"We gave it all away at the claims expo and had people coming up to us asking if we had extras." George beamed, looking pleased, which in turn, made me happy, too. A happy customer made for a happy me.

"Great."

"I really appreciate what you did for us," George gushed. "And I was wondering, would you like to have dinner with me?"

Now, he was just being silly. I would've worked hard to correct any error for any client. "That's nice, but not really necessary. Your business is—"

"Important, I know, and you have my business." He stared at me a beat with his somber blue eyes never leaving mine. "I mean…personally."

What am I missing here? And why is he looking at me like that?

"A date?" he managed, and then it hit me like a ton of online dating profiles. He was asking me out. George. The insurance company owner. Asking me out? Frankly, I'd never even *thought* of him that way before. Granted, I never looked at my clients as possible mates, but still. George was... Well, he was serious. Very serious. He didn't have much of a sense of humor, but he was always polite, always respectful, always on time. Basically, he was everything I often *didn't* look for in a guy.

George must have seen the uncertainty on my face.

"Unless you think it's inappropriate because we do business together..."

Maybe... Maybe the fact I didn't immediately want to say "yes" made him the perfect candidate. Dr. Susie was telling me *not* to go with my gut, even though it told me George was a little too...well... I glanced at his three-piece suit. Buttoned up. But I was learning not to trust myself, so...why not?

"No, I guess it would be fine," I said. Wouldn't it? "I mean... Yes, I think that would be nice."

Relief flooded George's features. "Great. I'll call you and make the appropriate arrangements."

Appropriate arrangements? That sounded a bit... formal. Too formal, maybe.

"Perfect," I said, choosing to ignore my gut, which was telling me a night with George was going to be the opposite of fun. But wasn't fun what had gotten me into trouble in the past? Maybe fun was overrated.

Ten

D ATE NIGHT WITH GEORGE CAME sooner than I'd expected, and as I listened to Dr. Susie to help me get excited about the date, I told myself I was doing the right thing. The grown-up thing. The *responsible* thing. That had to count for something, didn't it?

"Chivalry is not dead," Dr. Susie told me in her singsong voice on my audio book. "It's okay to expect and want a gentleman. We've come a long way, but we should still be treated like ladies. A real gentleman will do the big things and the small things."

Right, big. Like taking me to Denver's most expensive French restaurant for dinner, big. George spared no expense on our date. He'd picked a place even more impressive than I could've imagined— pristine white tablecloths, sterling silver cutlery, the soft glow of candlelight, and waiters dressed in suits.

One glance at the menu told me a single appetizer cost more than what I'd spent on food all day the day before. Every so often, the star chef, who had her own culinary show on the Food Network, walked through the dining room, thanking guests for coming. Usually, reservations were booked weeks in advance, and I wondered how George had managed to swing a table for two.

Okay, so maybe being a responsible grown-up had its perks. Like a three-hundred-dollar bottle of wine the waitress brought to us. She poured a sample for George to taste as they bantered back and forth in French.

"Parfait," George said after he took a sip and nodded his approval. "But you should really be tasting."

Well. Ooh, la la. That sure seemed the gentlemanly thing to do.

The waitress poured a little red wine in my glass, and I took a sip. Immediately, I realized why the wine cost three hundred dollars a bottle. It was, quite simply, the most amazing wine I'd ever tasted. I wondered if I spent more time with George, if I'd train my taste buds to recognize fine wine. I could get used to this.

"Wow, this is really...incredible." I knew the French were known for their wines, but...seriously, wow.

"Do you mind if I order for us?" George asked me.

I still felt too dazzled by the wine to even contemplate the menu, which I saw was entirely in French. Frankly, I had no idea what any of it said.

"Please do," I said, flooded by relief that I didn't have to bust out Google to translate. "You've done everything perfectly so far." Beyond perfect, really. He'd opened my car door, pulled out my chair, and complimented me on my outfit—a sleek blue dress and matching heels. He seemed to be following a checklist of "perfect things to do on a first date."

I listened as he began to order.

"Nous commencerons avec la salad Nicoise, suivi du steak tartar. Et comme plat principal nous prendrons tous les deux le canard a l'orange." He rattled off what I could only surmise was a delicious dinner in French.

The waitress nodded. *"Bon choix,"* she said. Then she turned to me. *"Est ce que je peux vous apportex quelque chose d'autre, mademoiselle?"*

"Oui. Oui." I nodded enthusiastically. I had no idea what I was agreeing to, but *"oui"* and *"bon jour"* were the only French words I knew.

The waitress, however, didn't leave. She stood, waiting, but I didn't know what she was waiting for.

George politely cleared his throat. "She wants to know if you need anything else," he said.

My face burned with embarrassment. For some reason, I hated for George to think I was out of my element. I couldn't say why. After all, I never went to fancy French restaurants, but still. "Oh! No, I'm fine, thank you."

The waitress smiled and then left our table.

"I didn't know you spoke French," I told George. It made me wonder what else I might not know about him. "That's impressive."

George shrugged, humble. "I just seem to have an ear for languages."

"Well, I don't," I said, thinking back to college when I'd nearly flunked Spanish 101. "And I just learned when I was in an Indian restaurant last week that *'naan'* does not mean 'no.'"

George smiled politely.

"They kept bringing me bread," I said and laughed at my own joke.

George, however, didn't seem to find it funny, or didn't want to laugh at my goofiness. But why not? It was funny. Wasn't it? I swallowed. *Ugh.* Did he think worse of me now? Also, why did that matter so much?

George seemed eager to change the subject. He raised his wine glass to toast.

"Well, to a beautiful—and the most interesting woman—I've ever met…and to getting to know her much better."

I suddenly felt hot and a little embarrassed. I wanted to say, *"Oh, seriously? That is so cheesy,"* but the utter look of seriousness on George's face told me that would be a mistake. He meant every word he said. And, the way he'd said it, so earnestly, made me want to *be* that person. That beautiful woman on a pedestal.

I could do this. I could be the alluring, interesting, complex woman he wanted, right? Maybe if I acted serious, I'd also be taken seriously. I clinked my glass against his. He stared at me with such admiration that I felt the warmth all the way across the table. Maybe George did deserve a second look. Maybe Dr. Susie was right. I could be a different woman, and maybe I'd get a different man.

"Cheers," I said, as our glasses clinked together.

The rest of the date sped by in the best dinner I'd ever eaten and in George being surprisingly lively company. I didn't laugh much, since George rarely cracked a joke, but we did talk about a range of issues, from politics to sibling rivalry, and he always gave thoughtful, interesting answers. I wanted to be more like that serious woman he saw in me. Maybe being a grown-up wasn't all bad, especially if it meant fancy dinners, serious conversations, and fantastic wine.

George didn't try to kiss me at my doorstep, but instead gave me a brief, business-like hug. It felt safe and appropriate, and I wondered about why I had absolutely no desire to take it any further. I thought about how I'd fought my inner teenager when I'd avoided kissing Robert. I'd not had to battle any urges with George. Wouldn't Dr. Susie say that was a good thing?

Yes, it was. I wouldn't let physical attraction cloud my judgment. For once, I'd make a romantic decision based on good sense.

Nadia called Saturday afternoon, Skyping to let me know she couldn't do our normal weekend walk with Duke. She was stuck at her house for another classroom emergency. Despite the fact that my nephew was just in preschool for three hours a day, three days a week, somehow, there still seemed to be a ridiculous amount of parent volunteer work involved. It made me rethink my plan to have three kids. Then again, part of me knew Nadia's type A personality could be to blame. She always insisted on doing things the hard way. Like now, for instance.

The preschool planned to hold a Healthy Eating Extravaganza to battle childhood obesity, and the school had bestowed the honor to dress up as fruits and vegetables to hand out fliers and amuse the kids on a few lucky parents. I felt it was kind of ironic since they'd *just* had a bake sale, but then again, maybe this was the school's way to make up for it: chocolate cupcakes one week, carrots the next. It all seemed to be for a good cause, but Nadia, as usual, made it far more complicated than it needed to be, insisting on sewing Michael's strawberry costume from scratch and then asking Mom to pitch in as she had only hours to go until fair time, and she still had to hem the bottom of the thing.

"Cass," Nadia began, shaking her head at me on-screen. "Listen to me and learn from my mistakes. Never volunteer to be room mother. One week, it's baking a hundred cupcakes, and the next, it's making costumes for the Healthy Eating Extravaganza."

I saw Michael wearing the worst strawberry costume I'd ever seen, Nadia relentlessly jabbing a needle in the hem.

"Ouch!" Michael bit his lip in pain. "I'm begging you…"

"Sorry," Nadia said, almost as an afterthought, despite having poked him—again. Poor guy. Michael had a heart of gold and the patience of a saint.

Mom popped her head on-screen. "You know, you could have ordered a costume on Amazon and had it here in one day. Free shipping with Prime."

"That's what *I* told her!" Michael flinched again when Nadia tugged hard on the hem of his strawberry costume.

"She's a walking advertisement now," I teased Mom, since everybody knew how much she loved Amazon. She wouldn't stop talking about Prime, even to clerks at the grocery store.

"Does this strawberry make me look fat?" Michael asked, preening in the oversized red berry.

"Yes," we all told him.

"That's what I thought." Michael gave an exaggerated sigh. At least he was having fun with it. Had to give him points for that.

"So...been dying to ask," Mom said, moving in front of the Skype camera. "Any more dates?"

"Actually, since I'm 'keeping my options open...'" I took a deep breath. "I went out to dinner with a client of mine, George Kazminski, and it was really nice. He was attentive and..." *Fun? No... Serious? Yes.* "A real gentleman. He held the door, pulled out my chair, and even ordered for us." *In French, mind you.*

Nadia perked up, looking at the screen. "Sounds like the type of man we're looking for."

"You mean *I'm* looking for," I said.

"Whatever." Nadia rolled her eyes and began fussing with the green collar of Michael's strawberry suit.

"I know I shouldn't ask," Mom said, trying to keep her voice low. "But...any sparks?"

I thought about the stiff hug at the end of the date.

"No," I said. "Not yet. But that's not what...*we're* looking for. Right, Nadia?"

Nadia offered a virtual fist bump to the screen. "Word."

I laughed a little, then Nadia told me she needed to run. The Healthy Eating Extravaganza began in fifteen, and they needed to get Mr. Strawberry to the school gym.

"How do I look?" Michael asked me.

Honestly? Kind of like a cross between the world's largest pimple and a mutant berry. I dared not say that.

"Really good," I lied.

As I shut off Skype, my phone dinged with an incoming message. I wondered if it might be George, but when I looked at the screen, I saw a missive from Robert. He wanted to take me out. *Tomorrow.* He was cashing in his choice of location for a second date. While he wouldn't tell me where we were going, he did tell me to dress for a long run.

That was about as far away as you could get from a fancy French restaurant. Still, curiosity piqued, I wanted to go. And, Dr. Susie *had* said to keep my options open. So, what was the harm?

Eleven

T**HE MORNING OF OUR SUNDAY** date, the autumn sky opened up and poured rain. It also happened to be my dad's birthday, a thought I pushed away almost the second it entered my head. *No sad thoughts today.* I had a date with Robert to look forward to, even though his "choice" for an outing turned out to include the Tri-County Sports Center and a row of treadmills.

"When you said, 'a running date,' I have to be honest, I thought you meant maybe outside with the sun shining, and perhaps bring the dogs…" I swiped my long ponytail off my shoulder and grinned at him, enjoying watching him squirm a little. We were both clad in work-out gear, Robert wearing one of his prized freebie shirts, and I happened to be in a tee bearing George's insurance logo. It had been partly an accident: I'd spilled coffee on the outfit I'd planned to wear, but while making the quick switch that morning, I'd figured the tee was a good reminder for me. After all, Robert wasn't the *only* man in the picture, and rather than just fall for his charm and that confident smile, I should keep Dr. Susie's advice in mind.

"That was the plan," he said. "And the weather forecast said it would be seventy-five degrees and sunny, but it's obviously not." He gestured toward the overcast skies out the windows. The forecast for an unseasonably mild week of weather had turned out to be dead wrong. "It's cold and rainy. I had a free pass for the gym, so I thought I'd use that for you." He wiggled his eyebrows. "I think that's romantic."

"It's so romantic." I laughed a little, rolling my eyes, and he did the same. Why did Robert feel so...comfy? Like my favorite pair of flannel PJs? I didn't have to worry about whether or not I sounded smart enough, or whether I was using the proper fork. Despite being in a rather dreary and run-of-the-mill gym, I found I didn't miss the violin music, the linen tablecloths, or the waitress speaking French from the night before.

"Now, let's see if you can keep up with me," Robert said as he jumped on a treadmill.

"Ooh, that sounds like a challenge," I said, knowing I was up for it.

"I don't know... I'm going to jam mine up...to

maybe six?" he teased. Six was a ten-minute mile. I usually ran an eight-minute mile, easy.

"Oh? That all?" I stepped onto the machine next to his and pulled out my ancient iPod, carrying my beloved REO Speedwagon. He saw it and raised a judging eyebrow.

"You're going to just put in earbuds from an ancient iPod?" he asked. "Guess that leaves me talking to myself. Good thing I agree with what I say most of the time. Wait..." He considered. "I don't."

A smile broke out on my face, because that just seemed to happen when Robert was around. "As luck would have it, I brought you earbuds and a splitter." I held up the extra buds. Sharing REO Speedwagon was actually *my* idea of romantic. Also, I wanted to test Robert. Would he be able to listen to a full song? Most guys weren't man enough for REO Speedwagon, in my experience. "You're welcome."

"Very considerate," Robert said and took the earbuds I handed him. "Thank you."

"Here we go," I said, cranking up REO Speedwagon's "Keep On Loving You" from 1980. "Motivation for our run."

The music began, and I flashed a smile at Robert, who was starting to look confused. I just snapped my fingers in tune as I began a slow warm-up jog.

"Seriously? You find...this...motivating?"

"It's REO Speedwagon! It's my mom's favorite band. She played it all the time when I was growing up." I didn't mention that she and my dad used to slow dance to this very song in our kitchen…a lot. Mom had one of those old boom boxes with a CD player, and she wore out at least two REO Speedwagon CDs. "Come on. You know you love it."

Because who doesn't truly love REO? Anyone who said they didn't was totally lying to himself.

"I *love* REO," Robert said, playing along. He started singing—badly. "I'm gonna keep on loving yooooou!" He threw in a goofy dance move and suddenly lost his footing. Before I knew it, he'd slipped right off the back of the treadmill. He took my iPod with him. It flew off the top of my console, banged against his still-moving treadmill, and got whirled backward. He landed with an unceremonious *thump* on his butt on the gym floor, and so did my iPod, hitting the ground with a sickening *crack*.

Shocked, I pushed the emergency stop button on my machine. "Are you…okay?"

"I'm fine," he said. He picked up my iPod, looking stricken. "Oh, I'm so sorry." A split in the glass ran across the entire front.

"What just happened?" I asked, seeing the broken screen, but not really wanting to let it in. *My iPod! The last gift I ever got from Dad.*

"I broke it. I'm sorry."

I picked it up, realizing the screen was destroyed. It didn't even light up anymore. Bad sign. *And on Dad's birthday.*

"Did you really hate the music of the '80s that much?" I tried to keep my tone light. After all, it was just a thing that could be replaced—and probably should have been by now. They'd made a score of new versions of iPods since then. *Not the one Dad gave me, though.* I swallowed tears. *No.* I wasn't going to cry. Dad wouldn't want that.

"No, I really didn't. I'm so sorry." Robert looked so pained. I felt for him. This whole second date of his planning wasn't working out at all like he'd hoped. "You must have been so fond of this. You've had it for two decades."

I laughed, because it was true. I thought about Dad giving it to me, wrapped up in a blue bow, after my high school graduation. But Robert looked so contrite, that I couldn't tell him *that* and add to his misery. It had been an accident. And like Dad used to say, *"Things aren't people, Cass. Things can be replaced."*

Still, I tried hitting play on the iPod, hoping maybe it would come to life, but it didn't. It was broken, probably for good.

"Should we have a moment of silence for this little

guy?" Robert glanced at me, unsure. "Is it too soon for jokes?"

I pushed aside the bit of sadness in my chest and said something Dad would have. "Not if they're funny."

"Ouch. Man pride stung. Speaking of man pride, there's a yoga class that starts in ten minutes. Should we?"

Since I didn't like the idea of running without REO Speedwagon, I nodded. Besides, seeing whether or not Robert could do a downward facing dog sounded like ample punishment for him. "Yes," I said.

"I'm sorry about your iPod," he said, truly meaning it. He stared at me a minute, and I felt that little electric current that had run between us on my doorstep the night of our first date. I almost thought he might lean over and kiss me, but then I realized I was the one doing the leaning.

No. No kisses. Not yet. Dr. Susie said keep the physical out of it until he's proven himself. And he just broke Dad's iPod!

"You should be," I said, but now I was teasing him. "Come on."

Robert lifted my mood during yoga by quite possibly being the worst in the class. He couldn't even touch his toes. When he'd told me he might be the least flexible man on earth, he wasn't kidding. But he put himself out there, made himself vulnerable—I

118

thought, mostly to get me to laugh. He didn't care if he made a fool of himself in front of the whole class. He was willing to sacrifice his pride to cheer me up, and it worked. I already felt better. If I'd been alone with my broken iPod, I might have slipped into a funk, but there was no way Robert would let that happen. He made a fool of himself in that class to make me smile.

Afterward, we walked through the gym parking lot in the drizzling rain, which had only just begun to slow. He'd parked far from the door, in the corner, near a large swath of trees. The Rockies loomed in the distance, though they were obscured by clouds today.

"The first thing I learned is don't trust the weather guy on Channel Four," Robert groaned as he glanced up at the sky.

"I don't know. I have to be honest. Seeing you flying off the treadmill? Pretty irresistible stuff."

Robert stuck his hands in the pockets of his zip-up windbreaker. "Yeah. It's my second date go-to move."

I chuckled a little at that.

"As is this." Robert popped up the back door of his SUV, revealing a picnic basket and a big flannel blanket. I couldn't believe it. Robert—funny, flirty Robert—was actually romantic. The gesture hit me as surprisingly sweet. I realized just how far off his plans had been when the rain started. He'd envisioned a whole other second date. To his credit, he hadn't gotten wrapped up in the disappointment. He'd soldiered on, even after falling on his butt *and* breaking my iPod. He opened the basket, revealing a Tupperware container of fresh fruit and pretty delicious-looking croissants. Tucked near the basket sat an oversized thermos he told me was filled with hot cocoa.

"A picnic?" I asked as Robert rearranged the back of his SUV, making room for the two of us to sit, the open door providing protection from the drizzle. "In the car? Well, you are just full of surprises, aren't you?"

"What would you like? Would you like fruit? A chocolate croissant?"

My stomach growled loudly in my own ears, expressing a clear vote for the croissant, but I knew fruit would be better. Healthier. Less carbs. No chocolate.

"I'll have the fruit," I said, proud of myself for going for the low-cal option. Take that, inner sweets monster.

"There you go," he said, handing me a container of strawberries and grapes. Already, I could feel disappointment seeping into my bones. I bet that chocolate croissant was amazing.

"Thank you," I said, reaching for the fruit as I eyed a croissant so full of chocolatey goodness the chocolate oozed out the ends. No. I'd be good. No carbs. No sugar. I sat down on the tailgate as he took a seat next to me. Our legs touched, and even through our workout clothes, I could feel the heat of his body. I liked it. *Sparks.* That's what Mom would call it. I somehow noticed every little movement he made. To distract myself from this new revelation, I opened the fruit container and ate a juicy grape.

"So, this is what I know about you," Robert began, glancing out at the rain-soaked conifers lining the road. "You have a dog named Duke. You like to run, and you own your own company, which is very impressive. What don't I know about you? Where were you born?"

"Right here in Denver," I said, thinking about the short version of my life. "I went to college in Boston. Then, right around my graduation, my dad passed away." No matter how often I said it, I never got used to that fact. I could still remember the phone call, the frantic sound of my sister's voice. *"Dad had a heart attack. He's in surgery. Mom is losing it. You need to come home."* I'd managed to get the first flight out, but I was too late. Dad died on the operating table when I was somewhere over Pennsylvania. I never even got to say a proper good-bye.

"So, I came back home to help my mom out." I'd felt so guilty for not being there, for not being able to say good-bye to Dad, for not being able to comfort

Mom, that part of me knew I'd never move away again. I'd never be that far away from my family.

"I'm so sorry," Robert said, dark eyes soft with emotion and empathy. I appreciated that. There was no good way to explain how it feels to lose a parent. "That's really sad."

I nodded. "Thank you." I meant it. Robert wasn't just funny and quick-witted. He was also kind.

"Were you guys close?"

I was surprised he hadn't abruptly changed the subject. Most men I'd dated hated talking about sad stuff. They'd much rather avoid the deep places. But Robert really wanted to know. He wasn't shying away from a tough topic.

"Yeah, we were," I admitted with a pang of sadness. "I was quite the Daddy's girl. He was the best. He would take me and my friends to concerts, ball games, the movies... And he knew how to disappear when I wanted him to—like at sleepovers and dances."

"He sounds like a great guy." Robert seemed genuinely impressed. I was grateful for that.

"He was," I said as Robert reached behind him to a grab a croissant from the picnic basket. "You actually remind me of him a little bit. He had that fun-and-adventurous thing. Like you. I really like that about you."

And he would've also made a fool of himself in yoga

to make me smile. He would've done anything to make me smile.

Robert stared at me a beat, and I wondered if I'd said too much. But then Robert just grinned, eyes warm. And I felt it again: those sparks, leaping back and forth between us like static electricity on a cold winter's day. I stared at him, and he at me. We leaned in closer, and I could feel the magnetic pull between us, a force beyond my control. I wanted to kiss him, badly. *Should I?* Dr. Susie would say "no." And I knew why. Because if I started kissing Robert, I had a feeling I wouldn't stop. Bye, George. Bye, *Dater's Handbook.* I'd fall so far down the rabbit hole I'd never find my way out. Because I knew, somehow, that kiss with Robert would be electric.

He moved closer, the croissant the only barrier between us, and then my nose got a whiff of buttery goodness. In a split second, my stomach decided for me, and I took a huge bite of his pastry.

"Unbelievable!" Robert cried. I wasn't sure if he was more annoyed that I'd detoured the kiss or stolen some of his lunch. But he chuckled, his eyes bright.

"I'm sorry," I laughed, relieved—yet, also a tad disappointed—to have avoided another kiss. "It's just so good."

"Stop eating my food!" he demanded, even as I snorted.

"I'll trade you," I said, handing him the heavy container of fruit. "I don't want the fruit."

He popped a grape into his mouth and sighed. "That's my favorite croissant, you know. My *favorite* one."

His puppy-dog expression just made me giggle louder as I nibbled on chocolate croissant. It *was* amazing.

Twelve

I FOUND MYSELF THINKING ABOUT ROBERT nearly nonstop for the next couple of days. It also didn't help that he was an ever-present fixture on my phone. He kept sending me pictures of food he might be eating, along with the lyrics from M.C. Hammer's "You Can't Touch This."

Two can play the cheesy music game, he'd texted me, causing me to laugh out loud. *I see your REO Speedwagon and raise you M.C. Hammer.*

Robert was fun and easy. It felt like I'd known him forever. Was it his playful humor that reminded me so much of Dad? Or was there some deeper, spiritual connection at work? Also, Robert asked if my mother and I were free for a surprise outing the following Friday.

Why do you want Mom along? I texted him.

To make sure you don't steal my food! Seriously,

though, I want to meet her. And ask her about your table manners...

Well, fair enough. Still, part of me wondered what was really going on. I'd never had a man ask me to bring my mother on a date. Curiosity piqued, I said yes.

Besides, it wouldn't interfere with my next date with George, which happened to be that very evening. To prep myself for George, I played Dr. Susie's book and listened to Chapter Seven.

"At this point, you may be getting close to someone," Dr. Susie told me in that ultra-confident, I-can-solve-all-your-problems voice.

True, I was. And that someone happened to be named Robert.

"Careful!" Dr. Susie warned me, her voice shrill. "You do not want to fall into old habits. Keep all options open as you figure out how you feel, what you want, and where you want to go."

That seemed like reasonable advice.

George planned to take me to a gallery opening, even though, truth be told, I had no idea what that even meant. Art gallery? I guessed so. I'd never been to one before—an opening or otherwise. I wore a nice navy sleeveless cocktail dress and matching heels. I felt grown-up and pretty. The pumps bit into my toes a bit, but that was the price I paid for dressing up. I glanced at my running sneakers in the corner of my bedroom, the same ones I'd worn for the date with Robert. How different could two dates be—or frankly, two men?

George arrived on time, as usual. I buzzed him up quickly while I finished putting on lipstick. He stepped into my place, almost as if unsure if he ought to. Duke trotted up to greet him, but George ignored my dog.

"You look beautiful," he told me, handing me a small bouquet of pink roses.

"Thank you," I said, taking the pretty flowers and smelling them. That was a sweet gesture. George glanced at my condo. "And...you have a very nice place. You must work hard to keep it clean, with... your dog." He glanced at Duke uncertainly.

Duke stared back. Was George not a dog person? Uh-oh.

"I hope you're not allergic," I said, wondering if that explained George's standoffishness to Duke. Robert took to Duke immediately, and he'd rescued a dog from the pound. If George hated dogs, that could be a deal-breaker. Duke wasn't going anywhere.

"No, I'm not. I just..."

Duke sniffed George's hand, and he pulled it back sharply.

"Never had dogs growing up."

"Oh, Duke's the best. He won't bite." I walked over and scratched my golden retriever behind the ears. "Go on, you can pet him."

George patted Duke awkwardly on the head. "Good boy," George said. At least he was trying. I figured with a little more exposure to Duke, he'd fall in love with my dog, who was the perfect canine.

"Ready to...uh...go?" George asked.

"Yes," I said and grabbed my purse from the foyer table. I nodded good-bye to Duke, who whined a little as we left.

A quick drive took us to the new art gallery. People dressed in various degrees of formal wear, from complete suits to khakis and ties, meandered through the art show as waiters passed around miniature quiches and other fine appetizers. Nobody spoke French, but the affair seemed just as formal as our dinner date had been. I found myself standing a little straighter, a little bit more on-my-toes. I knew next to nothing about art, and worried I'd say something dumb. I knew all about Pantone colors for marketing materials, but absolutely nothing about the Impressionists.

"So, how did you learn about art?" I asked George. Was he trying to impress me? I wanted to know. Or, did he really *know* art? If it were the former, then we could both giggle about not knowing anything about art, and then down the free glass of champagne and get on to food—the most important part of the evening. My stomach growled loudly in my ears.

"Before enrolling in the business program, I studied art in college," George told me. I tried to hide my disappointment. *Ack.* No sneaking out the back. This date wasn't just a stunt; he really liked this stuff. Okay.

"It gave me an appreciation for the way people look at things, the way humans express themselves."

I nodded, trying to think about something I could say. Did I mention I knew nothing—seriously nothing—about art? "I studied art for a couple of years," I said. "In preschool."

I smiled at him. He looked at me blankly. *You know, finger paints?* I wanted to joke, but didn't, because he probably wouldn't have gotten that, either. My joke was falling flat. I needed to change gears.

"It helped me...uh, learn about tactile senses," I said, trying to pretend my lame attempt at humor wasn't an attempt at all, but a serious approach to artistic sensitivity. "The way the paint would ooze between my fingers."

George ignored that comment. Ugh, I knew I'd sounded like I didn't know anything about art. Because...I didn't.

"This one really speaks to me," he said as we stopped in front of an abstract painting of an owl with yellow eyes besides big splashes of blue, red, and yellow paint. Honestly, my nephew could have done this with his finger paints, I was pretty sure. "The color choices, and the owl, front-and-center, acting as a symbol of wisdom, power, intuition, mystery, and change."

I nodded. Wow, he really saw all that? In…the owl?

"What does it say to you?" George asked, looking hopeful.

Eek. I looked at the painting, and I saw…an owl with oddly striped feet. That was pretty much it. Time for another joke.

"Hoo… Hoo… Hoo?"

At least George laughed this time. "That's… punny," he admitted as we walked away from the painting and deeper into the gallery. "How about this one?" he asked as we stopped in front of the next one. It was a mostly white canvas with streaks of black around the edges, a hint of orange, and a tiny bit of blue. Okay, this one gave me *nothing* to go on. Just a bunch of random lines and splotches. My nephew *absolutely* could have painted this —when he was just two years old.

George glanced at me, expecting an answer.

"Oh, I don't know," I said, and I didn't. What could I say? *It looks like a toddler did it.*

"Give it a try," George urged me, blue eyes so very earnest. "It's art. There is no wrong answer."

"Okay." I took a deep breath. I could pretend to be pretentious with the best of them, couldn't I? "I like the contrast of good and evil, the way the artist has created a dichotomy"—Ooh, Cass! A Boston College word—"of light and darkness, of day and night, illustrating the struggle of human nature, clawing from one moment of relief..."

I couldn't help but think if Robert were here, he'd totally tease me for this answer. Then, he'd play along, and we'd have a "pretentious-off." I glanced at George, ready for him to tease me—after all, how could splotches be good and evil? But he didn't.

"Interesting," George said, all seriousness. "Not sure the artist would necessarily agree with you, but everybody sees art in their own way..."

"I was just kidding," I said, wondering how often I'd have to spell that out for George. He looked confused, and for a second, it seemed he thought I was making fun of him. Then again, wasn't I? Now, I felt terrible. "No, I mean, I love abstract art. The form and shapes are really beautifully symmetrical. I didn't mean to make fun of it."

"It's all right," George said, looking a little relieved. "I didn't think you were making fun of it."

Oh, I totally was making fun of it.

"But we see what we see," George said, shrugging. "That's the beauty of art. Everybody sees what they want. Maybe this wasn't your thing. Maybe you prefer sculptures. Or not. There is no wrong. It's all okay."

This surprised me. I liked that George was so open-minded, so accepting of differences. He didn't judge me for not liking art as much as he did. George always seemed to prove sweeter than I gave him credit for. I wasn't experiencing those sparks yet, but maybe being sweet was more important in the long term.

"Thank you," I told him. "That means a lot to me."

Meanwhile, Mom couldn't wait to meet Robert. Though she didn't say it out loud, even I could tell she liked Robert better—his putt-putt date and picnic-in-the-rain date were better than George's expensive dinner and art gallery offerings in her mind. Still, even Mom couldn't guess why Robert had insisted she tag along on our third date.

Even better, he showed up to pick us both up in a stretch limo, complete with a stocked mini-bar inside. When she saw the limo in her driveway, I thought Mom's eyes might pop out of her head. She all but bounded down the walkway in her haste to get to the car. I'd rarely seen her move so fast when chocolate wasn't involved.

"I can't believe I'm in a limousine," Mom gushed

like a little girl and clapped her hands together as she slid in next to Robert. "Hello, I'm Gloria," she said, bubbling with excitement.

"Robert. Nice to meet you," he said and gently shook Mom's hand.

"This is so exciting, even though I have no idea where we're going," Mom said.

"That makes two of us," I said, glancing at Robert, who just grinned, mischief in his eyes.

"Wait, time out—a limousine ride isn't enough?" he joked. "Because this is all there is, ladies."

I could tell Mom didn't know if he was kidding or not. I knew he was.

"This is very nice, but I don't usually bring my mom on dates," I said. Mom nodded.

"Ah, well, actually, this is Gloria's date. You're just along for the ride. Literally."

"So *I'm* the third wheel?" I exclaimed.

"Yes. That's funny." He slapped his knee.

"Oh, come on, Robert. When are you going to tell us what the occasion is?" Mom was terrible with surprises. Christmas morning, she tore through presents faster than either Nadia or me. "The anticipation is killing me!"

Robert glanced out the tinted back window. "Well, we're almost there, so I guess I can tell you..." He paused for dramatic effect, and I thought Mom might faint. "We are going to a benefit concert for the Children's Hospital, and several musicians are…"

Mom and her eagle eye had already spotted the marquee out the window.

"REO Speedwagon!" she squealed in shock and delight.

"REO Speedwagon," Robert confirmed with a nod of his head.

"No!" How on earth had he managed this?

"No. But, yes." Robert pulled out three tickets and handed them to my mother. I thought she might faint with joy. A sly smile crept across his face. He was enjoying our shock, but I still couldn't believe he'd done it. I didn't even know they were on tour!

"I heard this was by invitation only." Mom looked both surprised and delighted. It warmed my heart to see her so happy. "These are impossible to get!"

"Our office helped set it up, so I asked for a couple of tickets…and then I asked for another one for the third wheel…" He pointed at me. Robert glanced at Mom. "Because I thought it would be weird if we went on a date without her."

"Wow," Mom said, unable to contain her excitement. "This is so incredibly sweet of you. I have loved REO Speedwagon forever, but never had a chance to see them live."

"Well, tonight's your night," Robert said. He grinned.

"Tonight's my night." Mom was happier than I'd seen her in…years. Her face lit up with joy. She so deserved this. She'd been through so much.

I felt my heart fill up with gratitude. Robert had gone above and beyond for Mom—and me.

The limo rolled to a stop near the VIP entrance, and as a worker opened our door, flashbulbs exploded. Mom giggled as she stepped out of the limo and onto the red carpet. Robert took my hand in his.

"You did this to try and score brownie points with Mom, didn't you?" I whispered.

"Me?" He looked shocked. "Why would I do that?" His face grew serious a moment. "Yes. That's exactly what I did." He stared at me a beat.

I squeezed his hand. Mom practically sprinted up the stairs ahead of us to get into the auditorium. "But now you have to listen to a whole night of REO Speedwagon," I pointed out.

"And that's going to be…awesome." He grinned at me. I grinned back. He was good. Very, very good. "I've decided to give in to the power of REO Speedwagon. Because…" He took a deep breath and began to sing. "*I can't fight this feeling…any longer.*"

Thirteen

MOM COULDN'T STOP TALKING ABOUT the "night of her life." Because Robert hadn't just gotten us *tickets* to the concert, he'd gotten us *fourth row* tickets. We could see sweat roll down frontman Kevin Cronin's temples. They sounded amazing, and I thought Mom might have a collapse from sheer joy. I had to admit, seeing them live, I was impressed. Robert gamely sang along with every song. It was the best night I'd had in…I didn't remember how long.

Mom kept repeating how incredible the show had been on the way home from the concert and when Robert dropped us both at her house. I'd already gamely planned to spend the night at Mom's, therefore avoiding the whole end-of-the-night-kiss scenario. It wasn't that I didn't want to kiss Robert. It was that once I started, I was pretty sure I wouldn't stop. I had to keep Dr. Susie's advice about keeping my options open. The sparks could not be denied. So my plan was to avoid that first-kiss scenario as long as possible—or at least until I was sure George was out of the running.

I'd never dated multiple guys at once. I was new at this, so I figured I might as well let Dr. Susie be my guide. After all, I'd been making the decisions in my love life for years, and look what that had gotten me: a series of terrible breakups.

A few days later, my non-milestone birthday arrived with little fanfare. Who cared about thirty-one? It was closer to thirty-five than twenty-five, which I didn't like at all. I think I missed my dad most on my birthday and Christmas. He always sang the "Birthday" song by The Beatles, complete with air guitar and goofy sound effects, and no matter how old I got, his performance always made me giggle. Dad used to tell me he'd sung the same thing when I was born, and the nurses had joined in, because that's the kind of guy Dad was. He could get a whole roomful of strangers to sing the Beatles…just because. He had a warm silliness that was contagious. You couldn't resist it, no matter how hard you tried. That's why he and Mom had been perfect together. Mom might have been far more reserved than Dad, but she appreciated a good joke better than anyone and wasn't afraid to poke fun at herself, either.

I woke early on my birthday and decided to take a predawn run on the treadmill. The mild weather had officially disappeared and snow now covered my favorite mountain paths, so I'd have to make do with my oversized painting of the Rockies in my apartment until the spring thaw. I played Dr. Susie from my iPad, my sole form of recreation since the untimely death of my iPod.

"Giving the right gift is imperative," Dr. Susie warned me. "Any gift should be personal *and* thoughtful."

Huh. I always thought the rule was "you get what you get, and you don't get upset." That was what Mom had always told me. But, turns out, getting the *right* gift might be more important than I thought.

"Good to know. Right, Duke?" I asked, as he walked on the doggy-mill next to mine. He didn't like this nearly as much as being outside. I didn't, either, but the fact was the snow was going to keep us in for a while.

An incoming FaceTime call from Nadia on my iPad came just as I'd begun my cooldown. It wasn't yet six thirty. I answered the ringing, and Nadia blew a paper horn and threw confetti at the screen.

"Happy Birthday!" she shouted. "And *many* more!"

"Aw, thank you," I said, feeling loved. Nadia and I might not always see eye to eye, but her heart was in the right place, and she loved me. What more could I ask from a sister?

"Am I first? Did I beat Mom?"

Ugh. I could ask that she not have this ongoing competition with Mom every year. Mom and Nadia knew I got a little down on my birthday. I didn't like aging, really, but more than that, I missed Dad, and they both knew it. Each one tried to outdo the other with early birthday wishes to take my mind off the fact there'd be nobody singing the Beatles' "Birthday." The one time Mom and Nadia had tried, I'd burst into tears, so neither one dared attempt the song again after that.

"Well, it's six thirty in the morning. So, yeah. You're the first."

Nadia did a little victory dance, pumping her fist in the air. "Ooh," she added, as if just thinking of it. "I can't wait to see what Robert and George get you."

"You're assuming they're getting me gifts." We'd only been on a few dates. Birthday gifts might be asking too much. Besides, I didn't even tell Robert it was my birthday, and the last I'd checked, men didn't have ESP.

"Uh…yeah. It's *imperative*," Nadia said, using Dr. Susie vocabulary. "If they don't, they're gone."

That might be a little too harsh, but I decided not to contradict her. Anything I said that challenged

Dr. Susie's wisdom would be met with full defensive retaliation by Nadia, and I had to get to the office sometime today.

My iPad lit up with another incoming call.

"Uh…I gotta go," I told Nadia. "It's Mom."

I clicked over to her. "Hi, Mom," I said, noticing she still hadn't quite gotten the hang of the camera in her phone. I saw her torso, her mouth, and her chin, but she held the camera too low to see the rest of her face, so the top of her head was cut off. I had to giggle a little. Technology and Mom didn't mix. Heck, it'd taken Nadia and me years to convince her just to *get* a smartphone.

"I know it's really early, but I wanted to be the first to wish you a happy birthday." She over-corrected the video picture, and now I saw most of the top of her head.

"Well, you are first," I lied, not having the heart to tell her otherwise. "Congratulations."

"Ha!" Mom pumped a fist in the air and sent the camera zooming around the room, nearly giving me vertigo. "Nadia always wants to be first, but she will never beat me now that I've mastered the video chat!" Of course, I was staring at a patch of carpet, but still. No need to tell her that.

"I'm very proud of you," I told Mom as she suddenly righted the video again and seemed not to know where to look. She gave me a big off-center smooch. "Love you!"

I headed into work hoping for an easy day, but immediately found no such luck. Once arriving at the office, I discovered that Phil had struck again. He'd ordered one thousand shirts with "Bank of Devner" on them. I had no idea what I'd do with the botched logos. Devner? Doesn't anybody spellcheck anymore? I was neck-deep in typos when George appeared at the office carrying a huge bouquet of flowers and wearing an enormous smile.

"I know you're working," he said, looking his crisp, pristine self in another three-piece suit. I wondered, briefly, how many he owned. "But I hope these brighten up your day."

He handed me the beautiful lilies.

"Oooh, thank you." I admired the white flowers and inhaled. They smelled good. "Lilies! My favorite. And you brought them *personally*." Dr. Susie would be proud. He'd nailed the personal touch when he could've simply ordered them online.

"Deliveries are so impersonal," he said, as if reading my mind. "And I wanted to wish you a happy birthday in person."

I took the huge bouquet and set it on my desk

behind me, seeing George in a new light. He never missed a beat. He always seemed to do the perfect thing, whether that was holding open the door for me or wishing me a happy birthday. I focused on his clear blue eyes, like the sky above the Rockies on a summer's day. Could there be sparks between us? *Maybe.*

"I know you're having dinner with your family tonight, but I look forward to celebrating with you on Friday."

Friday! That's right. He'd planned another date. I wondered what it would be this time. Opera, maybe? We'd done the art gallery already, and... I glanced at his crisp shirt and buttoned-up vest. I bet he did like opera. Mentally, I reminded myself to hit the dry cleaners. Whatever George had planned, I'd need a dress. And then came Saturday, with Robert. Had no idea what he planned, either, but given our putt-putt date, I knew whatever I had in my closet would probably be fine.

"I can't wait," I said. We shared a moment, and I wondered if he planned to hug me...in the middle of the office? I almost wanted him to. Yet, as the moment settled between us, George made no move...at all. I had to wonder...did *he* feel any sparks?

He cleared his throat. "Well, I'd better go," George said, deflating the moment. So much for sparks. "I have to be in a deposition in a half hour. Big accident dispute."

"Oh sure. Thank you again for the flowers. They are really beautiful." I smiled at George, and he smiled back. Just then, I saw Robert heading to us from the elevators.

Uh-oh.

Before I could usher George away, Robert had covered the short distance with his long legs, his wavy hair swept off his forehead, his well-worn, Sherpa-lined coat fitting his broad shoulders perfectly.

"Hi," Robert said, coming up behind George and peeking over his shoulder at me. "Is this a bad time?"

I sucked in a breath. *Bad time? The two men I'm dating...here? Yes, it's the worst of all times.*

George raised his eyebrows but moved away, allowing Robert to come between us. "Nope, I was just leaving," George said, tucking his well-manicured hands into the pockets of his wool coat. "She's all yours."

I am? I watched George retreat to the elevators without once looking back. He must've thought Robert was simply a client. Yet, he sure did cede his ground quickly. I wasn't sure how I felt about that. Relieved, definitely. I let out a sigh. The last thing I wanted to do was introduce the two men and then watch them shake hands. *"Robert, the fun-loving, rules-are-made-*

to-be-broken guy, meet George, the guy who never met a rule he didn't love, and never fails a Dr. Susie test." Ugh—my worst nightmare. Robert watched George for the briefest of seconds. George might not know he had competition, but I suspected Robert wasn't fooled.

"Hello," Robert said, stepping into my personal space. Instantly, I felt the sparks bouncing between us like tiny lightning bolts. He was so tall, so broad, and I suddenly wanted to put my hands on the firm front of his chest, feel the softness of his Sherpa-lined coat between my fingers. *No. Focus, Cass. Be on your toes.* He eyed the flowers for a beat and then me. Did he know George had given those to me? Had he seen? I grinned, nervous.

"Hi," I said, trying to distract him from the massive bouquet of lilies sitting on my desk behind me. *Those are not the flowers you're looking for,* I wanted to say and Jedi mind-trick him into not noticing. Why did I feel like I was cheating? I hadn't had the "relationship talk" with either man. Heck, I hadn't even *kissed* either one yet. Could you cheat on a man when you hadn't even kissed him? Still, my guilty heart hammered in my chest.

"I'm on my way to finalize the arrangements for this lantern festival I'm working on, but wanted to stop by and wish you a..." He pretended to shout. "Happy birthdaaaay!"

"How did you know it was my birthday?" I hadn't told him. I'd deliberately *not* told him. Why? I wasn't sure. I'd told George. Was I trying to give George a leg up? Was I sabotaging Robert? Or was I making Robert jump through more hoops because...I liked him more than I wanted to admit?

"Oh, Cass...Facebook, Google, Instagram, Twitter. There's a billboard on the highway, which, by the way, I think is too much."

I giggled, my face growing warm. Robert flashed his perfect, wry smile at me. "I know a lot about you. Too much, actually. The 'Rachel' haircut when you were a little girl? NOT good." He made a pitiful-sounding sigh.

"Wow." I shook my head, happy to slip into this flirty-teasing-banter thing we seemed to do naturally every time we saw one another. "You Googled me?" Secretly, of course, I was flattered. But I was going to give him *such* a hard time for that.

"No. I'm kidding." Robert grinned. "Your mom. She told me."

My mouth fell open. "Well, look at you two. You're BFFs now?"

"Yep." Robert slowly nodded. "She friended me."

"She *friended* you?" Now things were getting real. Mom barely knew how to work Facebook, so it was a miracle she'd managed that at all. Then again, if she'd friended Robert, she was serious about keeping tabs on him. "Wow. O-kay."

I made a mental note to have a long talk with Mom later about the dangers of friending men I'm casually dating. If I were a guy and some girl's mom friended me, I'd run for the hills. *Scratch that, the Rockies,* I thought, seeing their snowcapped peaks outside my office window.

"Anyway, I just wanted to give you this." Robert pulled out a box wrapped with a red ribbon. He handed it to me, and I found myself staring at a brand new pink iPod.

I blinked at it, remembering how Dad had given me my old one on the steps of the house I'd grown up in, on the day of my high school graduation. He'd made a goofy joke about how REO Speedwagon could get me through anything—especially college. Now here was Robert, giving me a brand new one. A tornado of different emotions swirled inside me, making me feel lightheaded. I was touched that he wanted to replace the one he'd broken, but also a bit sad, especially today because I missed Dad so much. This new pink one... could it ever replace the first?

"An iPod. That's pretty great." Why did Robert always seem to stir up so many different emotions? With George, I seemed to be trying to figure out if I *had* any feelings. With Robert, I seemed to feel them all at once. I never did well with the feels. Ugh. So much…feeling. Sad. Happy. Touched. I wanted to kiss him and run out of the room at the same time. What was happening to me? I didn't want to know. I hated introspection. I hated examining my emotions. So, I did what I do best. I deflected with a joke.

"But how did you know I needed a new one?"

"You know, I just had a feeling." Robert leaned a little closer to me, and at that second, all I wanted to do was kiss him. Though, I wasn't about to do that here in the office, was I? In front of my employees—and even Phil, walking from his desk to the coffeemaker down the hall. Robert, however, glanced at the clock on the wall in the office.

"I've got to go," Robert said. "I have a meeting with a paper lantern maker…so, I'm going to…" He touched my arm, and I could feel the heat of his hand through my sleeve. It felt good. I wanted to be wrapped up in that heat. I was drawn to him like a moth to a flame. *Just like all those other past mistakes.* No. I couldn't trust my instincts.

"Thanks," I called as he moved away. Just as he got to the door, he stopped and spun on his heel.

"No problem. Happy birthday. So I'll see you Friday? Is it Friday?"

Panic shot through me. Friday was George's night!

"No," I said a little too loudly, a little too forcefully. "Saturday. It's *Saturday*."

Robert's mouth curled up in a knowing smile. "Ah, right. Saturday." Did he know? Had he overheard George talking about Friday night? I swallowed, hoping I didn't look as guilty as I felt. He nodded. "Wonderful. See you then."

He didn't call me out on my double-booking of dates. *Phew. That was close.*

He nearly backed into Dana, who walked by him with a clipboard. "Ah, there's the bride."

"Hey!" Dana said, as Robert made his way out of my office. Dana spied the flowers on my desk. "Aw," she cooed. "Pretty flowers from Robert."

Er, right. Robert. I laughed uneasily as Dana kept walking to the copy room. I should correct her, but then, she might tell Robert I was dating George, and that could ruin everything. Ugh. How did I get into this mess? I didn't like leading a double life. I hadn't told Dana about George because I worried she'd be squarely in Camp Robert. Of course, why wouldn't she be? He was her husband's good friend.

My head felt like if it spun any harder, it might fly right off. George…or Robert. I wasn't sure which one I most wanted to see this weekend. Did that make me a bad person? Dr. Susie would say I ought to keep my options open, but now I was pretty sure Robert knew he had competition. Why did keeping my options open feel like cheating?

Fourteen

MY BIRTHDAY DINNER AT NADIA'S was everything I could've asked for and more. Nadia cooked me an impressive meal—I was never going to complain about farm-to-table, all-organic anything ever again. Mom brought out her own delicious, chocolate-frosting, double-chocolate layer cake that embodied all my birthdays for all time. The very taste sent me back to every amazing birthday as far as I could remember. My nephew, Jeremy, helped me blow out the candles. The four-year-old couldn't be cuter, and as he blew out the last one, Mom clapped.

"I hope all your wishes come true, darling," she told me, as she went about cutting the first piece.

"They will after I have a piece of this cake," I said, mouth watering. I could smell the chocolate decadence.

Mom began to cut a perfectly normal, perfectly average slice.

"Mom," I scoffed.

"Oh, right," Mom said. "Too small?"

"Of course." I let my inner sweets monster loose on my birthday. It only seemed fair.

"I forgot who I was dealing with here." Mom sent me a look telling me she might be a little proud of my inner sweets monster.

"We'll take that one," Michael said of the average piece. She plunked it onto a plate for Jeremy. "And we'll come back for seconds. How about you and I split this, huh, buddy?" Michael handed a fork to Jeremy, who nodded fiercely. "We're going to eat this and watch *Teenage Mutant Ninja Turtles*. My gift to you." He gave me a little bow. "Ladies' time."

Michael really took sweet to the next level.

Mom planted a righteous-sized piece of chocolate cake in front of me. Now this was more like it. I dug in with a fork and felt instantly transported back to my childhood. So good. Nadia—the very pregnant Nadia—waddled over and sat next to Mom, who gave her a piece, too.

"You're never going to believe what happened today," I told them between forkfuls of chocolate. "George and Robert *both* came to see me at work."

"No!" Mom exclaimed.

Nadia looked stricken as she leaned forward over her plate. "Not good. Did they meet?"

"No." *Not exactly.*

"Phew. Close call." Nadia exhaled and sank back in her chair. "But more importantly, what did they get you?"

"George brought flowers. Lilies."

"Oh, your favorite," Mom murmured, surprised. But she didn't exactly sound happy about it. Then again, she *would* be absolutely Team Robert, which would explain why she'd given him the heads-up about my birthday.

"Score one for George." Nadia seemed impressed. "Personal gift without being too over-the-top."

Mom was noticeably silent.

"And…Robert got me an iPod." I fished it out of my pocket and showed them the bright pink device. How could I explain how he'd gone flying off the treadmill when his dancing to REO Speedwagon had gotten too intense? I giggled a little at the memory.

Nadia frowned. "Electronics?" She said the word as if she was saying something gross like *spiders*. "You hate pink."

True, but Robert didn't know that. And…it was a personal gift—actually, the most personal gift I'd ever gotten. I wanted to tell Nadia this gift meant more than she knew.

"He knows that mine is broken," I said. *Actually, he broke it.* Though, if I said that, Nadia would nix him for sure. "And the pink is growing on me. And he got me a new one."

"Yeah, but you're not his *nephew.* I mean, an iPod really isn't personal."

Ugh. Nadia! I stuffed my mouth with chocolate cake so I wouldn't say something I regretted.

"Wait, why is an iPod not personal?" Mom jumped in, thank goodness. *Go, Mom!* "He knew she needed one, he got her something she needed—"

"Dr. Susie says—"

Mom barely contained an eye roll. "I don't care what Dr. Susie says. An iPod *is* an appropriate gift, and it sure will last a lot longer than flowers." Mom really liked Robert. *Really* liked him. Something told me this went beyond the REO Speedwagon concert, too. She was one-hundred-percent on Team Robert.

Did Robert remind her a little of Dad too? The thought made me feel that whirl of emotions again, so thick in my brain I almost felt dizzy. Focusing too much on Robert made me lightheaded. Maybe I shouldn't think about him so often. George didn't make me feel confused or off-balance.

"One thing that concerns me, though, is how long do you plan on dating both George and Robert at the same time?" Mom asked. "I don't think it's fair to either of them."

Ugh. The last thing I wanted to do was make a decision. Had Mom been talking to Robert? Had he told her he suspected about George? Double ugh.

"Mom's right," Nadia chimed in. *Here we go. The jump-on-Cass bandwagon.* "The *Handbook* was intended to weed out the wrong kind of man, not string multiple men along."

"Okay, but I'm not stringing them along." For goodness' sake, I hadn't even *kissed* either one of them yet. The most I'd done amounted to holding hands. How could that be misleading *anybody*? Of course, even I knew, on some level, Nadia had a point. I did feel a tad guilty about it.

"I'm getting to know them, and I don't want to make the wrong decision. Again." There. I'd admitted past guilt. Now, could we get off the bash-Cass train? I wasn't nearly ready to decide between the two men.

"Okay, but eventually, one of them is going to find out about the other," Mom pressed. Boy, she wasn't letting this go. "And someone's going to get hurt. Probably you."

What did she know? Was Robert thinking of bailing on me? I couldn't ask her, not with Nadia here. I'd never hear the end of it. Plus, if I interrogated

Mom, it would just give Nadia more reason to like George better. And I wasn't ready for that.

"Clearly, they both like you," Nadia pointed out. "But you're going to have to make a decision eventually."

I already knew this. "Okay, ugh." I hit the table in a gesture of crying uncle. "I'll make a decision already. But how?" The more I thought about Robert and George, the more difficult the choice became. Did I go for Robert and the tornado of emotion and fun he brought, or quiet, calm, grown-up George who seemed to see in me a person I sort of wanted to be—sophisticated, put together, in control, a person who liked art galleries and fine dining? I could be that person, if I tried hard enough. I just knew it.

"I think it's time we pull out the checklist," Nadia declared, pointing her dessert fork at me.

"Oh, there's a checklist." Mom sounded less than enthused.

"Yep, Dr. Susie has thought of everything." Nadia, on the other hand, appeared to be in her element. The type A personality thrived on lists, after all. "Here's the plan. You go out with George and Robert for another week and then we'll see how they rate, eliminate whichever one doesn't meet the requirements."

"I don't know." Mom shook her head. "I think it's

kind of weird to use a checklist to find love. I think it should be about the heart and…and feelings."

Feelings. The things I tried to avoid most of my life.

"Sure, if you want to end up with a Peter or a Jamie or a Jack." Nadia wrinkled her nose in disapproval.

Okay, no need to bring up ghost boyfriends of my past, thank you very much.

"Nadia's right," I conceded, even though I wasn't at all happy about it. "I've been following Dr. Susie's advice so far, and if I want to succeed, then I have to follow it through to the end."

I took another bite of chocolate cake. I was relieved to let someone else decide. Dr. Susie could take all the angst out of it. She'd decide for me.

Suddenly, I felt better already.

Dr. Susie's voice filled my small bathroom as I worked to get ready for THE date with George, the one that would determine whether or not he would be cast in the role of my boyfriend.

"It's decision time," Dr. Susie told me. "By now, you should know if the person you've been spending time with is worth elevating to the next level."

Of course, that was the thing. I didn't know who I liked more: George or Robert? If I let Mom decide,

Robert would win, hands down. He had the sparks, he had Dad's whimsical, adventurous nature, and he'd scored rare REO Speedwagon tickets and invited Mom. Could I really trust Mom's judgment? Nadia definitely put herself in Camp George, probably because she wished she could do more fine dining, given that she, Michael and Jeremy existed on a steady diet of dinosaur-shaped nuggets and carrot sticks. Then again, she was clearly biased, too.

So I couldn't take Mom or Nadia's advice. That left Dr. Susie. I fluffed my hair and studied my reflection. Was I really going to leave my love life up to a TV personality? I thought about making the decision myself. Funny, endearing Robert, and formal, educated, does-everything-by-the-book George. George would temper me, maybe, help me be more practical and keep my feet on the ground. How was I supposed to decide? Then I thought about having to tell one of them we were done. That made me even more anxious. No way. I couldn't do it. Let Dr. Susie decide.

"Some final things in our checklist to consider are…" Dr. Susie continued, unfazed on my audiobook. "How well does he know you? How much planning and effort has he put into your time together? And finally, does he respect your boundaries? You get to determine how and when a date ends."

"I got this, Dr. Susie," I said, switching off my iPod. George rang my doorbell right on time. I could practically set my watch by him. *That's nice,* I reminded myself. He was dependable and reliable, something I couldn't call any previous boyfriend, most of whom took being late to Olympic levels. Once more, I'd dressed up for George, wearing heels and a cocktail dress, and George wore one of his darker three-piece suits. Almost every time I'd seen him, he'd been wearing a suit. In fact, I wasn't sure I'd seen him in anything other than a tie.

I pushed the thought aside and decided to focus on the night ahead. George planned to take us to a classical quartet concert and a nice dinner out at a new, trendy gastropub—whatever that meant—in downtown Denver. It was a good thing I'd picked up my dry cleaning. I congratulated myself on thinking ahead. George took me places I'd never venture to on my own, so that was a good thing, right? I liked looking nice, even though sometimes, I felt like I might be playing dress-up. Normally, I lived in my gym clothes: yoga pants and oversized sweatshirts. But as he walked me into the ornate theatre with rows of pristine red velvet seats and other adults mingling around us, all wearing their finest, I had to admit I felt special. We took our seats and George handed me a playbill for the show.

I wondered what Dad would think of all this: the fancy dress, the orchestra seats. He wasn't exactly a classical music kind of guy.

"This quartet plays all over the world," George told me, voice low as he sat next to me. "You work so hard, I thought you would enjoy something soothing and relaxing."

I glanced at the solemn faces of the musicians in the program and wondered fleetingly if the music might be so relaxing it could put me to sleep. Honestly, I couldn't tell the difference between Mozart and Bach, and the last time I'd been to the orchestra was probably a sixth grade field trip.

"This will be a nice change of pace," I said. I could do this. I could be worldly and sophisticated and one of those women who owned a pair of opera glasses—wherever one might buy those. *Amazon, maybe? Probably.*

"But I thought you might not appreciate Bach or Tchaikovsky—too boring. This group is quite whimsical, and tonight, they'll be playing popular movie scores. Everything from *Lawrence of Arabia* to *Jaws.*"

"The theme from *Jaws*?" I bit off the joke bubbling up in my throat, the one that went something like, *Oh, good! So if I'm bored, I'll just think about a shark devouring me, and I'll wake right up.* No, I needed to take this seriously. I glanced at George's somber blue eyes. He did win points for trying to spice up classical music, and as the lights dimmed and the rumble of *Jaws* began, the chances of me falling asleep dropped to zero. As the quartet played, I found myself enjoying the music. I recognized every last score, and they featured some of my favorites including *Raiders of the Lost Ark* and *Batman.* I tapped my foot along to the familiar beats without even realizing it. George even reached over in the dark and took my hand. I squeezed his back, even as he quickly withdrew.

I wondered why he chose not to hold my hand longer, but as soon as the thought popped into my head, it disappeared as the quartet jumped on to another familiar tune, *Star Wars.* Oh, I liked this.

Intermission came in a blink of an eye and George led me out to the high-top tables near the concessions.

"Would you like some champagne?" he asked me, and I nodded quickly. He fetched two glasses of bubbles and a dish of chocolate-covered strawberries. Maybe he did know me. I took a bite of delicious goodness before I even took a sip of bubbly. George seemed to be glancing at me strangely, and I put the half-eaten strawberry down quickly on my napkin. Did I have a smudge of chocolate on my face? Or was I acting like a mannerless cretin who hadn't seen a decent meal—or dessert—in ages?

"Sorry," I murmured, self-consciously swiping the corners of my mouth with my fingers. "They're just... so good."

"Good." George grinned at me, the strange look gone, and I inwardly let out a breath of relief. I wanted to impress him. Then I remembered that *he* was the one who was supposed to be on trial here, not me. But why did I feel like it was my audition? I always felt so on display with George, like I had to be on my best behavior at all times.

I nudged the chocolate berry. "You sure know a way to a girl's heart," I said. *Because chocolate is most definitely the way to mine.*

George's features softened, his stark blue eyes staring intently at me. "I certainly hope so." He held up his champagne glass. I scrambled to do the same. *Yes, normal people toast before they stuff their face with chocolate-covered strawberries, Cass.* Sheesh.

"Cheers, Cassandra," he said.

Cassandra. The name rubbed me slightly the wrong way, but I let it slide. Nobody called me Cassandra. But this was the *new* me, right? The Dr. Susie me—a sophisticated woman with grown-up tastes.

"Cheers." I clinked my glass against his. We took our sips and then I focused on devouring the rest of my strawberry—and four more. George joined me, eating the remaining three without complaint, until the lights flicked on and off, announcing the performers planned a return to the stage soon.

After the show, George took me to the swanky new restaurant downtown called Slate. No French on the menu this time, but it might as well have been in another language. Gastropub seemed to mean *everything you never knew you could eat and couldn't pronounce anyway.* What was "quark"? Or "massaged kale"? Did that mean the greens got a deep tissue massage before they came to my plate? And there were so many compotes and purees...more than I could count or understand. What *was* a "pure fingerling potato and barley compote"? Yet George read the menu with ease, seeming completely at home, while I felt terrified of opening my mouth and saying something stupid like, *"What's 'deconstructed truffle ravioli'?"* A billion jokes popped into my mind, but I silenced every one. I knew if I made fun of the menu, George wouldn't find that amusing, and worse, he'd know I didn't belong here.

And I belonged, didn't I? When George looked at me, he saw a woman of refined tastes, and that was what I'd try to be. We sped through dinner, my head buzzing with fine wine. Despite not knowing exactly what I ate, the food was delicious. Thankfully, when dessert rolled around, the chocolate cheesecake looked completely familiar and tasted perfect. Yes, I could get used to such upscale dining with George. No doubt about it. Though, as the meal wound down, I found myself thinking about how this date might end. In my mind, the *Jaws* theme song was never far.

Duh...nuh. Duh...nuh.

As George drove me back to my condo, a million thoughts darted through my head. Was I ready for... the next big step? Should I kiss him? Dr. Susie would say no. Would he make the first move? He'd barely touched me the whole night—except for the quick hand squeeze during the concert. Were there any sparks at all? Surely, I owed it to myself to find out. My worry about the end of the night circled below us like a shark. To kiss or not to kiss? Should I invite him up for coffee, and then see?

No, I decided. After all, I had a date with Robert tomorrow. The very thought of seeing Robert made my heart speed up. I had no doubt about sparks with him. But hadn't sparks gotten me into trouble in the past? Time for me to start thinking first and feeling later. Feelings just got me in trouble.

George pulled into the visitor's parking spot and then rushed over to get my door—the perfect gentleman, as usual. I smiled as I climbed out of the car. He didn't take my hand, but he did walk closely with me to my door, our fingertips nearly touching. The cold air made our breath come out in tiny puffs, and the chill seeped through my coat. Snow crunched under our feet as we stopped on my porch, and suddenly, the sky filled with snow flurries.

We paused at my door, and I turned to look at George as we stood between the decorated conifer trees. Holiday lights twinkled near us, and the whole setting felt so very romantic. I glanced at George, at his earnest blue eyes. Handsome? Check. Polite? Definitely. But I wondered what would happen if I ruffled that always-perfectly-coifed hair.

"Well, I guess this is good night. That was really fun going to the string quartet," I said, and I meant it. "I never would have chosen that, but it was nice."

Maybe that was George's superpower: he could open my horizons, make me try new things.

"Well, I could tell you enjoyed it because you've been humming the theme from *Jaws* since we left," he said and grinned. "It's very sweet."

Uh-oh. Had I been humming *Jaws* out loud? I giggled nervously. I glanced at George and realized he still felt like a stranger. Here I'd been worried about drawing boundaries, but now, face-to-face with George on my stoop, I had no trouble with self-control. That was a good thing, wasn't it?

"Uh, I'd invite you up, but... I just..." What should I say? *"But, I've got contestant number two waiting in the wings for tomorrow and I'm not sure you've passed on to the final round."* No. *"I'm suddenly feeling like you're a perfect stranger"?* No, that wasn't right, either.

"When you're ready," George said without even a hint of disappointment. "I'm not going anywhere."

I felt an immense wave of relief. *He's not going anywhere.* Dr. Susie would love that. Reliable, dependable George. No-pressure George. Suddenly, I felt so grateful. I liked him much more in that moment. I stared into his clear blue eyes, so serious, and I felt the urge to kiss him. Perhaps this might be the very first spark. He moved closer, and so did I. Yes, the first kiss. The first spark. I'd find out, finally, if there might really be a future for us. Our lips were so close now, all it would take was a few more inches and then... Suddenly, George shifted and wrapped me in a hug—a friendly, but a little stiff, not-too-tight hug.

What had just happened? I'd thought we were on the road to make-out town, but suddenly, we'd taken a hard right to the friend zone. What the heck?

George pulled back, oblivious to the lost moment of passion, and smiled. "I'll text you?"

"Yeah, good." I nodded my head quickly, like a bobble doll and then fidgeted with my keys. I darted inside and George waved through the glass door front as he turned and headed back to his car. I smiled weakly. *Awkward.* Why did I never quite feel on the same wavelength with George? He went right, and I went left. He wanted to hug me, and I was thinking about something decidedly more…romantic. Maybe that just meant we didn't know each other well enough yet. After all, we'd only been out a couple of times, and while he'd been a client forever, that was a business relationship.

But why did our personal relationship feel so businesslike?

I tromped up the stairs to my condo, shaking snow off my jacket. Well, we still hadn't kissed yet. There *could* still be sparks, and I almost thought I felt one there on the porch, so George still looked to be in the running.

Of course, Robert could always blow him right out of the water tomorrow night.

Suddenly, the theme song from *Jaws* popped into my head again, and I hummed it as I ducked into my condo and shut the door behind me.

Fifteen

ROBERT TEXTED THE NEXT DAY and told me to feel free to dress casually, and I couldn't believe how relieved I felt. My poor pinched toes had grown two blisters from my heels the night before and were dying for a little comfy-sneaker time. Besides, snow blanketed the sidewalks, and heels would be less than practical. Now I could wear my warm lined snow boots and jeans without fear of being underdressed.

I found myself looking forward to time with Robert. He always made me laugh, and I never felt like I had to censor myself or roll out my best table manners, which was a welcome change. I wouldn't have to figure out which jokes he might find funny, or whether I'd look like an idiot if I asked what *foie gras* was. Was that goose or duck? Oh, I never could remember.

Robert told me he planned to take me to a place

he knew I'd love, but when he pulled into the diner parking lot, I nearly laughed out loud. A diner! It was off the beaten path a bit and open twenty-four hours, not the kind of place for a lot of foot traffic during prime time on Saturday.

Inside, the diner was brightly lit with faded furniture and country music blaring from the speakers. The older couple sitting at the corner table and the black-and-white checkered menus almost made me feel like I'd stepped into a Norman Rockwell painting. The restaurant looked nearly empty. Based on their "sunny side up" breakfast special and "world-famous coffee," they probably got more traffic at breakfast time. A waitress stood in the corner, pencil behind her ear and white apron around her middle. Meanwhile, the diner's manager, wearing a flannel shirt and hiking boots, walked by and told us to grab a seat anywhere.

This restaurant seemed to be the exact opposite of George's pick the night before. This one had garish fluorescent lights and paper napkins. Slate had offered up expensive, modern seating and mood lighting, as well as a wine list that boasted two-hundred-dollar bottles and up. I didn't even think the diner served wine.

"You have no idea how long the wait is to get into this place," Robert joked.

"I can only imagine," I said. George had told me

it usually took months to get into Slate. I didn't know why Robert had picked such a casual place, but so far, I was all for it.

Robert helped me out of my coat.

"I almost called to make a reservation," he said as he hung up my jacket on an empty rack by the door.

"Did you?" I laughed, thinking the waitress with the pencil behind her ear probably wouldn't find that funny. "Let's sit at the counter." If we'd come for the ultimate diner experience, we might as well try out those vinyl-covered stools. *So relieved I can actually read the menu.*

"So," I said, glancing around. "What's on their wine list?"

"Oh, well, you're in for a treat." Robert looked at the drink specials tent card on the counter. "They have Bud Light, vintage 2017, as well as a Denver craft pilsner, that I'm told has bright, fruity flavors and a smooth, crisp finish."

"How can I resist that?" I laughed. How I wished I could've taken Robert to Slate. We would've laughed ourselves silly during the whole meal.

"*Garçon*," Robert called to the manager, who now manned the counter. "Two of your finest glasses of pilsner."

The manager nodded and grabbed two bottles of beer from the fridge behind him and popped them. "Glass or no glass?"

"Glass, of course. We're not savages," Robert deadpanned.

The manager poured us the beers, and Robert clinked his glass against mine. "Cheers," he said, and we took a deep drink. It wasn't fine champagne, but then again, with Zac Brown Band blaring in the background, the beer just seemed...right.

I glanced at the menu and was relieved to see no signs of "massaged kale" or any compotes or purees. Sure, I'd liked the fancy food at Slate, but it had also made me feel a little uncomfortable. I'd spent the whole night with my back straight and rigid, like I was sitting in a church pew.

"Hey, boss," Robert called to the manager. "What are your specials tonight?"

"We have a steak salad," he said. The way he said "salad" made me think he wasn't a fan of greens. "But... we are known for our wing sampler." He tapped the menu with pride.

I thought about the chocolate-covered strawberries *and* cheesecake from yesterday, not to mention all the other rich food I couldn't pronounce from Slate. I decided I ought to take it easy today. Go for the healthy, low-carb choice.

"I'll take the steak salad," I said, proud of myself.

The manager whistled, as if to say, *You sure about that?* Yes, I was sure. I was going to eat healthy. Even though wings sounded delicious. Wings, I reminded myself, also happened to be Peter's favorite food. *No more backtracking.*

"And what do you recommend?" Robert asked, giving me a sidelong glance.

"The wing sampler." The manager didn't hesitate. He *really* didn't like greens.

"Okay, I'm going to make it easy on you and get the wings," Robert said. He glanced at me. "Five *bold* flavors of wings. Have you ever heard of *so* many flavors on a chicken body part?"

"I can't say that I have."

"Right." Robert nodded slowly, deliberately, his dark eyes playful. "Which makes me think you're going to eat my wings."

The manager hung by, notepad in hand, probably anticipating we might be changing our minds about what to eat.

"No," I said, shaking my head. "I ordered the steak salad." Even at the word "salad," the manager rolled his eyes. "That's all major food groups in just one salad, so we're good." The manager frowned, now reading from my face that we weren't going to take back the salad and order another plate of wings instead.

"I doubt it." Robert shook his head. He didn't believe me! Like I was some kind of out-of-control food thief. I'd prove him wrong.

"Um, sir," Robert called out to the manager. "Can you save us a piece of the Seven-Layer Tower chocolate cake…because you don't want to know what happens to you if you don't."

Wait…seven-layer chocolate cake? Robert won my full attention. I sat up straighter. The manager nodded and scribbled it down on his notepad.

"You're serious?"

"Yes, I am." Robert flashed his bright white smile. "They're famous for their cake." He tapped the menu. Somehow, I'd missed the declaration of "World-Famous Seven-Layer Chocolate Cake." Robert read some of the description in an exaggerated announcer's voice. "Seven layers of chocolatey heaven… Can you climb the tower?"

"Oh, well, I didn't wear my hiking boots, but if it's chocolate, it's on." I grabbed my fork and held it like a spear. Clearly, Robert knew how to talk directly to my inner sweets monster.

"Look at that," the manager said, shaking his head and looking doubtful. "Confident."

He sounded like the chocolate cake really was as tall as the Rocky Mountains. Well, massive or not, I could handle it. I took a swig of beer, and so did Robert.

"So… How was your night last night?"

I nearly choked on my beer. Did Robert know I'd

been out with George? "Um, good. I…uh…went out to dinner with a friend."

"Friend." Robert raised one eyebrow. Had he been talking to Mom? Something about the way he looked at me said he knew more than he let on. Still, I wasn't about to confirm his suspicions. What would I say? *"Uh, yes, I went out with my other suitor, and now you better bring your A game."*

Robert turned a bit, and his knee grazed mine. I felt heat there, a sizzle of electricity. No lack of sparks here. I wanted to jump into his lap and kiss him until neither one of us could breathe. Did he feel the irresistible tug between us, like two planets, unsure of who had the stronger gravitational pull? He grinned at me, and in that instant, I knew he did.

Somehow, when it came to Robert, I didn't have to debate whether or not to kiss him. I studied his full lips, quirked into a knowing smile. *No, Cass. Behave. What would Dr. Susie say?*

Since we and the elderly couple in the corner were the only guests at the diner, our order came up quickly. The manager slid my steak salad and Robert's amazing platter of wings, which smelled delicious, in front of us. I took a bite of the salad, and it did taste good, but…one whiff of Robert's wings—a mix of sweet, spicy and tangy—and instantly I regretted my order. Robert dug in, looking satisfied as he bit into a succulent chicken wing.

Yeah. Okay. I wasn't going to be able to stay in my lane. I had to admit I'd made a horrible mistake with the salad. I should've taken the cues from the manager. Now Robert's food tempted me with the aroma of all things scrumptious.

The manager delivered Robert's basket of fries, and while Robert seemed momentarily distracted as he dunked a fry in ketchup, I reached out and stole a spicy barbecue wing. Robert just froze, French fry in midair, and stared at me, shaking his head. A slow smile crossed his face.

"Wow, that is amazing," I said, enjoying the spicy, sweet perfection.

"Uh, yeah." Robert moved the basket between us, closer to my sticky fingers. "Here. There are five bold flavors, you might as well compare."

I giggled a little. What was it about Robert that made me want to steal his food? And oddly, what made me *not* want to steal George's? I realized that I had no idea how George would react to something so…improper.

"Oh, I plan on it," I said. Robert laughed, deep in his throat, a rumble I felt in my own belly. Boy, did I love making that man laugh. I wanted to do it again.

I reached for another wing and happily munched. Sweet, gooey awesomeness.

I swallowed another bite. Wow, this *was* good. I'd nearly finished the whole thing when I felt an itch in my throat. Heat flared up the back of my neck. I started to see spots. My tongue was swelling up…

"Cass…are you okay?" Robert asked me as the manager brought us the largest slice of chocolate cake I'd ever seen. "You look…"

"Red, green, and pale all over," the manager said, his eyes growing wide. "Let me get you a wet towel." He set down the cake and scurried to the kitchen.

"Cass…you have a rash." Robert swung his hand across his neck. I glared at the wing bone. Was that sweet goodness…honey?

"Wait a second…was there…" I stood on shaky feet, the restaurant starting to swirl as my throat seemed to close. I had a knife in my hand, but Robert took it gently, as if I were a toddler with a sharp object. I must look even wobblier than I feel. "Was there honey in that?" I fumbled for my purse. EpiPen. I needed my EpiPen. But the reaction was coming and I was getting dizzy. It was harder to breathe.

"Yes, there…"

I tried to reach the EpiPen, but my purse toppled over and onto the floor before I could get it. The darkness closed in on me, and I fainted.

I woke up in the back of an ambulance, my heart racing, the siren wailing, and Robert's worried face over mine.

"There she is," Robert said, grabbing my hand. The paramedic checked my blood pressure as we hurtled down the street. I was lying on my back, strapped to a gurney, feeling every bump in the road.

"What...happened?" I managed.

"Honey happened," Robert declared. "Why didn't you tell me you were allergic to honey?"

Then I remembered stealing Robert's honey-laced chicken wings. And then reaching for my Epi, but not getting to it in time.

"Usually, it's not a problem."

"Cass! You went into anaphylactic shock." Robert glanced over at the paramedic, who was uncuffing the blood pressure roll from my arm. "He said you could've died."

The paramedic gravely nodded.

"I had an EpiPen in my purse..."

"That spilled on the ground along with the wings *and* the fries. When you go down, missy, you take everything with you." Robert grinned at me and I flashed him a rueful smile.

"How's your head?" the paramedic asked.

"Fine, I think." I had a headache, and I felt like

I'd just run a marathon, but that was the same heady rush I usually got when I got an epinephrine shot. It was pure adrenaline, after all. I glanced at my shirt and saw a blotchy red stain down the front of my new white tee.

"What's that?"

"Ketchup," he told me. "You took the fries down and all the silverware. It all happened so fast. I tried to catch you but missed, and then when I got down on the ground to see if you were okay, one of the customers thought I'd stabbed you. He called 911."

"Maybe I should start calling you Michael Myers. Or Jason."

Robert grinned. "Maybe. But thank goodness he did call. The paramedics were there in less than two minutes. Seriously, are you okay?"

"Yeah, I'll be fine. The hospital isn't necessary," I said, feeling like my cheeks were on fire. I'd had the honey allergy since I was a kid, and while Dad made a point of telling me I shouldn't be ashamed of it, I still felt a little embarrassed. All the kids I knew had peanut or shellfish allergies, not *honey*.

"Are you kidding? I've always wanted to ride in an ambulance. I mean…this is awesome." Robert made a sound like a European siren. The paramedic glanced at him oddly.

"I'm ruining our date, though."

"Nobody's ruining anything," Robert told me. "And...the manager wrapped up the cake to go." He held up an enormous Styrofoam container. "When the doc gives you the green light, we're going to climb the chocolate mountain."

"Oh, good." I grinned. I felt better already.

We arrived at the hospital a short while later. They wheeled us into an exam room in the ER, where we stayed for a couple of hours. It had been awhile since I'd ingested any honey. Usually, I was good about avoiding it, and even when I did eat some, normally I was on it with the EpiPen. But this time, I'd missed it. Probably because I'd been distracted by Robert's amazing dark eyes and his deep laugh. I'd had three whole bites before I'd even realized I was in trouble.

The doctor wanted to keep an eye on me to make sure that, after the epinephrine wore off, the reaction didn't come back. It was standard ER procedure for food allergies, and I remembered it from the last time I'd had a trip to the ER, back when I was twelve.

Robert sat at my bedside, where he'd remained for several hours. I'd told him he didn't have to stay, but he'd insisted.

"Doctor, would you tell this young lady that she shouldn't steal other people's food?" Robert asked the man in the white coat. "It could be deadly."

The doctor just shook his head as he scribbled on his notepad. "I wouldn't recommend it."

"See?" Robert said.

I laughed a little. "Hey, that's cold!" I pretended to whack Robert, but he ducked.

"Tell you what. Why don't I just not order honey, and then you can steal anything you want from my plate." He paused a beat, and I nearly drowned in those sweet brown eyes. He'd give up honey for me *and* he'd let me share all his future meals? It was all so...unbelievably thoughtful. The thudding of my heart in my chest had absolutely nothing to do with that Epi-shot. It had everything to do with Robert.

"Okay," I said. Suddenly, I liked the idea of stealing food off his plate for weeks, months...maybe even longer. I realized only Robert could make a trip to the ER fun.

Eventually, the doctor came back in, checking the clock.

"Well, Cass, I think you're free to go," the doctor told us. "I don't think you have a concussion, but you did hit your head on the fall, so just take it easy tonight, okay? If you experience dizziness or vomiting, call us immediately, okay?"

I nodded. It was just a little bump on the head. I'd be fine.

"And no more honey, okay?"

"No danger of that. I learned my lesson," I said, as I hopped down off the exam table, eager to get out of my hospital gown and back into my clothes. I hadn't checked my makeup and had no idea what I even looked like: blotchy, swollen, and red no doubt. I probably looked ridiculous.

"Come on," Robert said. "I'll drive you home."

We took a cab back to the diner, where Robert's car waited for us, and then Robert drove me home, despite me insisting the cab would be just fine. I still felt the sting of embarrassment—it's not every day a girl goes into anaphylactic shock on a date—but Robert insisted he was just glad I was okay. He also kept cracking jokes, which made me feel better.

When we got to my condo, I realized I hadn't even thought about what to do once we got here. Invite him up? Try to kiss him good night? Then again, why would he want to kiss me with my red, splotchy, hive-covered face and too-puffy lips? I scratched my neck, which was still sore and inflamed. It would be swollen for a day or two. I felt the opposite of sexy. Honestly, I just wanted to crawl into bed and forget this whole date had ever happened. What a nightmare.

We stopped at my front stoop, and I paused, looking up at Robert's face. Why did he have to be *so* handsome? Seriously, he was so kissable in that moment. Meanwhile, I got a glimpse of my reflection in the glass door. I felt like some kind of alien monster: blotchy, red, and so very swollen.

"Thank you for riding in the ambulance to the emergency room," I said.

"It was a date for the memory books," he said, shaking his head. "No, I'm just sorry tonight turned out the way that it did. Can I...have a redo, please?"

He wanted a redo? I was the one who needed the redo. *Look* at my face! I could feel how bad the swelling was. I avoided glancing at the glass reflection. I didn't need to see that horror show again.

"Yes, absolutely, we'll give it another shot." I nodded quickly. At least he wasn't already making excuses about *not* seeing me. Amazingly, he was still interested.

"I know you're capable of taking care of yourself, but I would feel better if I stayed. Just to make sure you're okay."

He looked so serious and earnest in that moment. It was considerate, but I also just craved alone time so I could lick my wounds, and let the Benadryl finally kick in so my face would return to normal.

"That's really sweet, but all I want to do is sleep." *Sleep and forget that this night ever happened.* "I really just need"—*to have the ground open me up and swallow me so this embarrassing date can end*—"to sleep."

"I'm not trying to be weird, I promise. I'll keep my

hands to myself," Robert assured me. "It would make me feel a lot better. You did hit your head…and that was my fault. I didn't catch you."

"Catch me?" I shook my head. "How were you supposed to know I'd faint?"

"Well, normally, my reflexes are better than that. Women faint around me all the time." He grinned, showing he was kidding, and I giggled a little. "I mean *this* face. Come on."

The way he said it made me chuckle.

"Okay," I said and sighed. I knew by the determined look in his eyes that I didn't have the energy to argue. "But you're sleeping on the couch."

"I'd *insist* on it. I've got my reputation to protect," Robert teased, and I laughed again. Part of me had to admit I liked the idea of him being here. I mean, I knew I was fine. But what if I had hit my head harder than I thought?

We walked upstairs to my condo, and when I opened the door, Duke greeted Robert like an old pal. Robert scratched Duke behind the ears. "You need to go out, boy?" he asked.

Right. He would. I glanced at the leash near the door.

"Mind if I take him out? You can rest." I felt an immense wave of relief. My head did hurt, and taking

Duke out in the cold wasn't at the top of my list of things I was dying to do.

"Would you? That would be great. I usually take him to the small patch of grass in back."

"No problem. I'm on it." Robert snapped the leash on Duke and led him out my door. I couldn't help but remember how awkward George had been with Duke. Robert was clearly a dog person. I didn't even have to remind him to get the plastic doggie bags, which were sitting in a roll in the bowl by the door.

Him taking care of Duke felt strangely like something Dad would do to make sure I could rest. It felt nice to be cared for. I'd been on my own for so long, even when I was in a relationship, that I'd forgotten what that was like.

About ten minutes later, Robert brought Duke back in, and my dog settled happily in his bed. Robert asked if I wanted hot cocoa and set about making us some. I could feel the EpiPen wearing off. One second, I felt hyped-up and wired, and the next second, all the life drained out of me, like the world's biggest sugar crash. I yawned. My eyes suddenly felt heavy. Really, all I needed to do was sleep.

I lay down, and before the kettle even whistled, I'd fallen asleep.

When I woke up, just after dawn, Robert was already gone. No note, no nothing.

Had he woken up and realized his mistake? How completely unromantic and ridiculous the whole evening had been?

I yawned and rubbed my face. In my hallway mirror, I saw the swelling had gone down in the night. Still, my hair looked a fright. Maybe that was why Robert booked it on out of there. But why no note? No text, even?

My spirits sagged in disappointment. Ugh, what a disaster. He'd seemed so interested, but everyone knew what sneaking out before dawn meant. *Let's not make this permanent good-bye awkward.*

Well, no chance of making a lasting good impression then. I swung open my refrigerator door and saw the giant Styrofoam container with the chocolate cake.

At least he left me that. I grabbed a fork from a nearby drawer and decided to drown my sorrows in chocolate.

Sixteen

NADIA AND MOM MET ME for dinner Sunday to evaluate the two contenders who'd had callbacks for the role of My Boyfriend. I'd told them both about the honey exposure, only because I didn't want them to freak out—which they would—if I sprung the ER visit on them over dinner. They both wanted to make sure I was okay, and I was, though I had to admit my pride still hurt a bit. How embarrassing: fainting on a date! It was no wonder I was single.

Mom, Nadia, and I sat in a cozy corner next to a roaring fireplace at a bar near Nadia's house. I scoured the menu, checking and double-checking for honey. I didn't want any more close calls. The waiter brought us a bottle of wine, poured two glasses, and fetched Nadia her requested cup of hot tea. Nadia took out her hardbound copy of *The Dater's Handbook* and flipped to Dr. Susie's dreaded checklist at the back.

I took a long sip of wine. I might need many more sips soon. Which man won more of Dr. Susie's checks on the list? Frankly, I prayed it did not point to Robert. After he'd scuttled out of my place without a word or even a text, I was almost convinced he'd taken *himself* out of the running. But I'd promised to let Dr. Susie decide, so I needed to see it through.

"Okay, I've got the checklist ready. Let's see how the guys did," she declared. I glanced at Mom, who did not disguise her disapproval of the whole process. She eyed the list as if it sported eight legs and venom.

"Question one. 'Does he make adequate plans for the evening?' Let's start with George." Nadia looked at me expectantly.

"George took me to a concert," I said.

"I like concerts," Mom managed, clearly not liking giving anything to George.

"A classic quartet," I added.

"Not so much," Mom said, taking a swig of her wine.

"I know...you think classical music would be boring, but they played themes from famous movies like *Jaws*. It was actually really fun."

Mom stared at me like I'd been possessed. Nadia nodded and scribbled notes in the margin of her book.

"But why didn't you just go to a movie?" Mom wasn't going to like *anything* George did. Of this, I was certain. Robert's bribe of REO Speedwagon tickets couldn't be overcome. How could I explain to Mom, who hated all things snooty, that classical concerts can be fun?

"Because," Nadia intervened. "He put effort into it. He considered her likes and planned ahead. And she liked it. Point, George." With a flourish, Nadia made a checkmark on her list.

"Okay, now what about Robert?" Mom did not bother to disguise her clear favoritism.

"Okay, well, Robert started out strong," I said, dreading getting to later on in the date when I was on a gurney in an ambulance. "He took me to this diner—well, his favorite diner—"

"A diner?" Nadia wrinkled her nose. She hated greasy spoons.

"Ooh, did they have that counter and the stools? I love those places," Mom exclaimed. The waiter brought some cheese sticks and Mom dug in.

"They did," I said. "And they were known for chocolate cake."

"Your favorite!" Mom pointed out, clapping her hands. She seemed so excited about this diner that I almost wondered if *she'd* helped Robert plan the outing. For all I knew, they could've been plotting together on Facebook.

"No," Nadia said, shaking her head. "I'm not

sure about Robert's restaurant choice. It's a date. He could've picked something a little nicer. George took you to a concert—"

"Where they couldn't *talk* to each other," Mom argued. She put down her wine, a little too forcefully, and it sloshed in the glass.

"Nope, I'm going to say *no check*." Nadia pressed her lips together in disapproval. I knew that stubborn look, and so did Mom, who let out an exasperated sigh. "Next question." She skimmed it. "Oh, this is a big one." She glanced up at me. "'Is your date genuine? Is he being true to himself or his he putting on airs to impress you?'"

I thought about this. Both men seemed very genuine. I thought of George's earnest appreciation of classical music, and then Robert's goofy sense of humor. Besides, neither one would've lasted this long if they'd been pretending. I can smell fakers a mile away. Which was also why Robert's disappearing act this morning had sent a signal as clear as day.

"Ugh!" Mom glared at the ceiling, reaching the limits of her patience. "So *bor*-ing. Is there anything good on that sheet? Is there anything about romance?" She nibbled on some more cheese.

"Fine," Nadia said, running down the list for a different question. "Skipping ahead... 'Is the evening romantic throughout?'"

I considered this a minute. Was the time spent with George romantic? Renditions of *Jaws* and then the odd, platonic hug? Well, I guessed that could be romantic. Under certain circumstances. Maybe.

"Well, yes, I think so. George's date included champagne and chocolate-covered strawberries—" I didn't even get to finish my sentence before Nadia leapt.

"Another check," Nadia declared gleefully as she put another mark by George's name. I almost thought Nadia might want to date George.

"What about Robert?" Mom cried, once more sticking up for her Facebook friend. "And the food at that diner? I bet their chocolate cake was amazing. Diners always have good dessert."

"Well, I was trying to be good and ordered the salad, but he got the diner special, the chicken wings. 'Five amazing flavors.'" I imitated Robert's exaggerated voice. Mom grinned. "I'm not proud of it, but I ended up stealing some of his."

"That's romantic! He let you share his food." Mom glared at Nadia.

"Well…except that one of his wings had honey on it. Thus, my trip to the ER."

"Unfortunate," Nadia said, clicking her tongue in disapproval as she tapped her pencil on the checklist. "Another point lost for Robert."

"Come on." Mom wiped her mouth furiously with a napkin. "There was no way he could've known about her allergy. And she ate off *his* plate."

Nadia glanced at Mom and arched a knowing eyebrow. Then she flipped to the next page and began reading aloud. "'By now, he should know all about you...'"

Mom grunted. "Oh, you know what? I was married to your father for twenty-six years, and he couldn't tell you what I liked on my hot dog. Didn't mean he didn't care."

That much was true. Dad loved Mom to pieces, anyone could see that—whether or not he remembered what condiments she liked. Besides, I'd never told Robert about my honey allergy. How else would he have known? I didn't know many people who asked that question first on a date. *Are you, by chance, allergic to honey?* It's not exactly a common thing.

Nadia took a diplomatic sip of her hot tea. "Okay, we'll agree to disagree on that one. Let's go back to the list and the final question. End of date. 'Does he respect your boundaries?'"

I thought back on the weekend.

"George absolutely respected my boundaries. Maybe a little too much." I told them about the almost-kiss turned into platonic friend hug.

Mom looked shocked. She put her wine glass down. "He *hugged* you?"

"I wish it weren't true."

Mom just *tsked* and shook her head some more.

"He was being respectful," Nadia said, glancing down at the book. "Point George." She scribbled another mark by George's name. George sure was getting a lot of checks. How did I feel about that? I wasn't even sure.

"Respectful, yes," Mom agreed. "Romantic? No." Wow, Mom was pushing Robert hard.

"Okay, look, but it was nice. I'd say it *was* romantic up until that point," I said, wanting to defend George. Mom wasn't giving him a chance at all.

"Let's move on to Robert," Nadia said.

"Yes, let's. *Please*," Mom agreed.

So, I told them about how he rode in the ambulance with me to the hospital.

"Point, Robert," Mom said. "And, also, you should've *called* me. I am your mother."

"Mom, I didn't want to worry you. I was fine."

Nadia and Mom exchanged looks.

"Anyway, I told Robert to go home, but he insisted on coming in. He was worried about me."

"That's sweet. Very considerate. What happened?" Mom leaned forward, eager for the details. Like I'd tell her if anything *really* happened.

Nadia clucked, shaking her head.

"We both fell asleep. Nothing happened."

"But what about this morning?" Mom asked, hopeful.

"No. When I woke up, he was just gone. No note... Nothing." I twisted my hands in my lap. This was the part I hated to admit. He'd abandoned me.

Nadia shook her head, making disapproving sounds. "That is a serious infraction," Nadia said, unable to hold her tongue any longer. "Boundaries breached. First, you wanted him to leave, and then he stays overnight, and then he leaves without even saying good-bye?" Nadia glanced at her list once more. "I hate to say this, but it's not looking good for Robert."

"Oh, come on," Mom argued, her cheeks getting a bit red, either from the wine or from her temper. "It may not have gone perfectly, but he was really trying."

"Not hard enough," Nadia said, and I had to admit, part of me agreed with her. Why hadn't he said good-bye? Had I been too much trouble, after all?

"It was *one* bad date," Mom exclaimed. "Cass," she pleaded with me. "You have to admit there's something between you two. I saw you guys. You can't tell me you don't have feelings for Robert."

So this wasn't just about the REO Speedwagon tickets.

"I do," I admitted. "I like him. I really like him."

Too much. Him bolting from my place in the predawn hours had hurt more than I wanted to admit. I'd come to rely on him. He was taking care of me, and then he was gone. Just like Dad—except Dad didn't leave me by choice. I felt those dark, sad emotions bubble up inside me and I pressed them down again. Hard.

"Well, that's all that should matter," Mom said, as if I'd proven her point. But she had it all wrong. This was why I couldn't count on guys like Robert. This was why I never got serious about anyone, because they could leave me at any minute.

"No," Nadia declared, and I thought Mom might actually throttle her firstborn. "According to the *Handbook,* there needs to be more. There needs to be consistency and reliability."

Mom snorted. "That's great if you want hugs for the rest of your life." Her sarcasm was thick. "Tell me something, when you look into George's eyes, does it feel the same as when you look into Robert's eyes?"

Well, no, of course not. With George, I had to force myself to think about what comes next, and with Robert, everything seemed so easy. *When he was around, that is,* I reminded myself. That was before he pulled a Houdini this morning.

"Those feelings fade," Nadia declared and glared at Mom. I wondered if that was why she was pushing George so hard. Did George remind her of dutiful, reliable Michael? "When you have kids, and you work, and you have to sew strawberry costumes late into the night, and Michael gets home tired, and…"

Mom and I glanced at one another and then back to Nadia.

"Okay, this is not about me, but I think I've made my point."

"Mom, I completely see what you're saying." I took a deep breath. How could I explain to her that as excited as Robert made me, he also terrified me? How could I explain that him bolting this morning had shaken me to my core? I remembered how Mom was when Dad died. I never wanted to be that vulnerable, that helpless. If I let Robert in, truly, I'd be giving him the power to hurt me in just that way. I wasn't ready for that. Not now.

"I've had these feelings before," I said. "And they've gotten me nowhere. I don't want to make the same mistake over again. I like George and I like Robert. It's not fair to either of them. I have to make a decision."

And I thought I already knew what that would be.

Seventeen

Fog shrouded the Rocky Mountains as I glanced out the window of my office around seven o'clock Tuesday night. Everyone, including still mostly clueless Phil and hard-working Dana, had gone home for the day. Robert had texted me a quick, *Hope you're feeling okay.* It was nice, true, but why had he waited more than two days to check in with me? I hadn't heard a peep from him on Sunday after he'd snuck out of my apartment, and nothing on Monday, either, and now...this. I need someone who will be there for me, someone I can count on.

I'd had plenty of time to mull over my feelings, and after dinner with Mom and Nadia, I knew what I needed to do. So, why did it seem...wrong? I thought about texting him the bad news, but I knew that wasn't fair either. I owed him at least a phone call.

Robert picked up on the first ring. "Hey!" He

sounded excited to hear from me. Then again, maybe he wasn't sure who this was.

"Hey, it's Cass," I said quickly.

"Cass…yeah. I noticed." I could almost feel his grin from the other end of the phone. But if he was happy I called, why had he snuck out? Why had he waited *two days* to check in on me? No time for wondering about that now.

"How are you? I hadn't heard from you, so—"

"I was thinking," I said, interrupting him. If I didn't get this out now, I never would. If he cracked a joke and made me laugh, I'd lose my nerve. At least I wasn't looking at him right now. Those brown eyes? That squared-off chin? That thick brown hair? In person, I'd never be able to break up with him. Did that make me a coward? Probably.

"I've been thinking and…" I took a deep breath. *Just say it.* Rip the bandage off already. "I don't think we should see each other anymore."

Dead silence met me on the other end of the phone, and for a second, I thought we'd been disconnected.

Then Robert spoke. "You're sure about this?" His voice sounded flat. Distant. Was he angry? Or maybe even relieved? Maybe he snuck out of my apartment that morning because he didn't really like me as much as I liked him. That thought hurt more than I wanted it to.

"Yeah," I said. "I'm sure." But I wasn't at all sure. Dr. Susie's checklist said George had won, but my gut told me I was the one who was losing.

"Okay," he said. That was it. He didn't fight. He seemed ready to step out of my life with no resistance at all. It proved he didn't really care. Not as much as I had about him.

"I'm sorry," I said.

"Yeah, okay." Now he sounded brisk, busy, distracted. "Well, then, this is good-bye."

He hung up and I stared at my phone. Why didn't I feel more relieved? I wanted to cry.

Why did he seem so fine with it all?

Because you were breaking up with him.

Didn't Dr. Susie tell me that I deserved someone who would fight for me, like my own knight in shining armor? Didn't I deserve someone who *chose* me, worked hard to be with me and win my affection? I'd told Robert to go, and he had, but if he really cared for me, wouldn't he have fought to stay?

I spent the next week walking through my life like a zombie. Everything seemed to remind me of Robert. We got a new client asking for personalized colored golf balls, and I thought about our putt-putt date. A near miss with honey-mustard dressing on a salad one day at lunch made me think of the ambulance ride and the horrible third date. Still, I had to put him behind me. I needed to focus on George.

The nice thing about George, I reminded myself, *is that he isn't threatening.* He didn't make me think about Dad or what I'd lost when he died, or how Mom nearly fell apart then, or how, if I truly let myself be vulnerable with a man, I'd be risking the same thing. George felt safe, comfortable, and most of all, I could keep that storm of feelings buried, locked away.

Besides, I needed to focus more on the positives in my life, so I'd stop dwelling on Robert.

Instead, I focused on incompetent Phil. He seemed to actually be making progress. During my usual morning meeting with Dana, he popped into my office, beaming, proud to show us the prototype of the *new* Tornadoes *fútbol.*

"I like it," I said, examining the mini *fútbol.*

"Pretty good, right?" Phil looked so proud he could burst.

"Good color scheme, nice font size, good placement. It's the *right* type of *fútbol.* Dana?" I asked as I handed her the prototype.

"Yeah, looks good." She glanced at me. "*Finally,*" she murmured, though Phil hardly seemed to notice.

"Let's get them into production."

Phil clutched his iPad to his chest. "I'm *so* on this,"

he declared, bubbling with enthusiasm. He rushed out of my office but then skidded to a halt and made a quick U-turn. "Wait—how many?"

Dana glared at him. I pursed my lips. *Really, Phil?*

"A thousand," Dana prompted him.

"Right. I should've known that." He smiled anxiously at us, like a puppy dog eager for approval. Poor Phil. Baby steps for him. He bustled out of the office once more.

"That was due, like, three weeks ago, right?" Dana asked me, tossing the little ball in the air.

"Yes," I sighed. "But his dad was really good to me when I was starting out, and I wanted to pay it forward with him."

"All right," Dana said, voice wary. But Phil *was* making progress. I'd make a decent employee out of him yet.

George called me then, a welcome distraction.

"Just wanted to make sure I have the time right for tomorrow," he said, always concerned about punctuality. "It's two o'clock?"

"That's right." My nephew's birthday party started promptly then. "Are you sure you're up for this? Meeting my family? *And* not to mention a house full of preschoolers hyped up on sugar?"

George didn't laugh. "Of course I am, Cassandra. Meeting your family is a great honor."

He sounded like a commoner accepting a knighthood. Also, there was that "Cassandra" again. I cringed whenever I heard it. I was trying to get used to it but, ugh. I just didn't like it. I wanted tell him I preferred Cass, but he'd been saying "Cassandra" for so long by then that it would be awkward. Maybe he'd pick up on the contextual clues when he heard my entire family calling me Cass.

I said, "Well, trust me, you might not feel that way *after* you meet them."

Nadia, of course, would fawn all over him, but I worried Mom might not be such a fan. I actually hadn't told either of them I'd broken up with Robert. I decided to bring George as a surprise, but the closer I got to the party, the more I thought I might be making a mistake.

I'd told Nadia I was bringing a friend, and despite all her grilling about which friend, I'd managed to keep it a secret. Mom had been pinging me on Facebook Messenger all day, trying to figure out who was coming with me, but I'd not cracked. They'd both just have to wait and see.

The suspense is killing me, Mom had written, and I knew it was, because she was notoriously impatient and hated surprises. But I didn't want to give Mom a heads up. If she knew I'd broken up with Robert, she'd be mad, and honestly, I didn't want to have to go over, in fine detail, how Robert seemed content to let me go. That fact still stung.

Mom could handle the George surprise, right? And Nadia would help. Nadia was George's biggest fan.

"I can't wait to see you tomorrow," George said.

"Me too," I said, wondering if that were true. Well, I needed to introduce George to Mom, Nadia, and Michael and hope for the best. I'd have to disappoint one of them, at least, maybe more. Nadia had told me Michael was secretly hoping I'd get back with Peter because he missed the free wings every Friday night.

I'd just have to trust Dr. Susie to see me through. She'd steered me right so far. I needed to finish this.

Saturday came, and so did one of early winter's first blizzards. The near white-out conditions made me worry that George might cancel, but instead, he showed up at my doorstep right on time, his four-wheel-drive SUV ready to tackle the snow-covered roads. He'd even bought his own gift for my nephew.

"A children's illustrated dictionary," he told me, as he patted the wrapped gift. "Every kid needs one, and this will help improve his vocabulary. They say the most important learning years are ages zero until five."

"Oh, uh…that was sweet," I managed, secretly glad I bought a mechanical robot dinosaur with light-up eyes that roared when you pressed a button. It was just the kind of loud, obnoxious toy that Nadia hated and Jeremy loved. It was my duty as the world's best aunt to spoil my nephew *and* annoy my sister at the same time.

I glanced at his open coat and was relieved to see he hadn't worn a three-piece suit, which would've been out of place at a five-year-old's party. He wore a stiff-collared shirt and a blue cashmere sweater. Still a bit nice for preschoolers, but I appreciated he wasn't wearing a vest. In fact, this might be the very first time I'd seen him out of a vest. He looked good in business casual.

I grabbed my coat and hat and said good-bye to Duke. Outside, George helped me into his SUV, holding the door open for me as I hopped in. He drove impeccably in the rough conditions. The snow meant fewer people on the roads, and we managed to get behind a salt truck on the expressway, which made our trip less slippery. George parked in front of my sister's house, and we scurried through the snow to her porch. I rang the doorbell, heart thudding as I worried about how Mom might react. *Please let her be okay with this.*

Michael, wearing an apron, a sherpa-lined aviator's hat, and an oven mitt, opened the door. He was clearly on barbecue hot dog duty, despite the snow. His nose and cheeks were bright red from the cold. Behind him,

I could see their house, decorated from floor to ceiling in dinosaur-themed party goods with a giant T. Rex balloon bouncing in the corner of the kitchen. Nadia had gone all out, not that I'd expected anything less.

"Cass," he cried. Then he noticed my date.

"And…George," I added, nodding at him.

"George? George," Nadia clapped her hands together as Michael threw open the door and we stepped in, stomping our boots on the all-weather rug.

"George?" I could hear Mom ask in the background, sounding none-too-pleased as she rounded the corner from the kitchen. She frowned, and I gave her a warning look. *Be nice,* I mentally scolded. Mom managed a weak smile. I made the introductions, and George shook everyone's hand. Mom, however, retreated quickly to the kitchen and busied herself with getting the platter of hamburgers and hot dogs ready. Clearly, she had no intention of getting to know him better.

"Nice to meet you," Michael said.

"Can you get more dino-dogs going, hon?" Nadia asked him, and Michael's shoulders slumped.

"More? Oh…" He glanced at the blizzard outside. "Okay. I'll be back." He smiled at me.

"I'm so glad you made it," Nadia said, stepping in as Michael lumbered away. "I know a dinosaur party isn't high on most people's weekend to-do list."

"It's nice to meet all of you," George said and gave

a sort of short bow, all stiff and formal. "Cassandra has been telling me quite a lot about you."

"And it's great to meet you—finally." Nadia smiled.

Finally? Really, Nadia? We'd gone out on four dates! It had been six weeks, not six months.

"Cass has been telling us all about you. String quartet? Impressive." Nadia rested one hand on her swollen belly.

"No, *this* is very impressive," George said, gesturing to the kitchen and dining room, all decked out in dino-decorations. "A dinosaur cake, pin the tail on the brachiosaurus, feed the T. Rex..." George shook his head.

"And outside, we have a Jurassic jump house," Nadia said with mom pride. She knew she'd nailed this party, and she planned to take all the credit.

"Yes, because apparently, Jurassic is in again," Mom said as she put the giant platter of food on the table. She wouldn't even make eye contact with George. Was she this upset that I didn't pick Robert? Well, of course she was. I knew that. But I hadn't expected her to take it so personally. She kept studying the food, and moving plates around, not even seeming to be up for conversation. This was going to be a long afternoon.

"Well, George hasn't met the birthday boy yet," I told Nadia. "We're going to go do that." I led George away from my now-antisocial mother and went off to find Jeremy.

Jeremy was playing with a bunch of oversized plastic dinos with his friends in the den. "Cass!" He jumped up to hug me. "Did you bring me a big present?"

"The biggest," I assured him.

"Yeah!" He pumped one fist in the air, though I noticed a look of disapproval crossing George's face.

"Uh, Jeremy, this is my friend, George."

"Hi." Jeremy gave him a curt wave.

"Actually," George said, "what we should say when we meet someone new is, 'Nice to meet you,' and shake hands." George showed Jeremy how to shake hands. "That's how real gentlemen do it."

I felt a ripple of unease. Why was he correcting my just-turned-five nephew? He hadn't been rude, and saying "hi" was perfectly fine. Next, he'd be telling Jeremy he needed to ditch his dino T-shirts in favor of vests and ties.

"Nice to meet you!" Jeremy shouted and shook George's hand once more, a little harder than he should have, probably, and with a little too much enthusiasm. George frowned. If he corrected him *again,* I'd have to say something.

But George let it slide. I scolded myself. He was just trying to help, right? He meant well, and Jeremy didn't seem to be offended. He trotted back to his friends to begin another plastic dino battle. Maybe I was overreacting.

As we made our way to the kitchen, Michael tromped in from outside, stomping snow on the mat and carrying a platter full of newly barbecued hot dogs.

"Hey, Cass. George." He nodded at us as he tugged off his oven mitt and put it on the kitchen counter. "So, George. I suppose congratulations are in order?"

Uh-oh. I bit my lip.

"Okay." George looked confused now. "For what?"

Abort, Michael. Abort. I glared at him, but he missed my look altogether. *Clueless!* I nudged Nadia. *Do something,* I silently shouted.

"Well, you've passed the tests, beaten all the other suitors, and now you've been declared the winner. Well-played, good sir!" Michael bent at the waist in an exaggerated bow.

No, no, *noooooo.* Please, ground, open up and swallow me whole.

"Sorry," Nadia blurted quickly, scooting over to Michael. "He's pretending to be a king fighting dragons, all that medieval stuff." She glanced at him and gave him a short elbow to the ribs. "Honey, this is a dinosaur party. Not dragons. Remember? There are no suitors!"

Michael frowned. Then he glanced at me, and apparently seemed to finally get it.

"Oh. Riiight. There are no suitors. Of course! Of course, there's no suitors." He looked at George, and George looked at me. Oh, boy. This party was not turning out how I'd planned. "So, George. Maybe you could help me hang the dino piñata in the living room?"

"Oh, good. A piñata," George deadpanned. "Just what the kids need. More sugar." I laughed uneasily. Michael took George by the arm and steered him into the living room. *Please let him not bring up Robert, or anything else that will get me in trouble.*

Sorry, Nadia mouthed to me, but I shrugged. I knew Michael hadn't meant any harm. And as I watched the two men try to figure out where to hang a piñata indoors, it was kind of comical. Eventually, they both gave in and opted to tie the candy-filled dino to a broomstick and dangle it above the kids' heads. Jeremy, as birthday boy, got the first hit. Nadia blindfolded him with a handkerchief, spun him around twice, and then put a wiffle bat in his hands.

"All right, Jeremy," Nadia told him, letting him go. "Give it a good whack."

He thwacked hard at the blue and red dino, but missed the first time. Then his blindfold slid down.

After that, he swung the bat and made contact: a hard hit, though the piñata stayed intact.

I laughed. Nothing like taking advantage of an advantage.

"The kid's got a nice swing," Mom said, probably already planning out a lifetime of Little League. Both Nadia and I played softball for years. Jeremy hit the piñata again.

"It's a lot easier without a blindfold," George commented, crossing his arms across his sweater and clearly looking as if he disapproved. "And kind of cheating, don't you think?"

Cheating? It's a living room piñata and the kid's birthday!

"He's a kid." Mom turned, the beginnings of a frown line forming between her eyes. "It's all about the candy."

Her tone left no room for argument, though George didn't take the hint. Jeremy swung once more.

"I suppose," he said, as the piñata burst open and candy rained down on the cheering kids. They dove to the carpet to snatch up handfuls. "Still, it's a good teaching moment. After all, cheating won't get him very far in life…"

I thought Mom might grab the wiffle bat and take a swing at George.

"Did someone say lava juice?" I intervened quickly

as I saw the steam coming out of Mom's ears. "I would *love* some more."

I took George by the arm and led him to the refreshments table and away from Mom's glare. He didn't realize I'd just saved his life. Mom was sweet as pie until you threatened one of her cubs—or grandcubs—and then Mama Bear came out to fight and it wasn't pretty.

We had more lava juice—strawberry milk—as well as dino dogs, and the party wound down pretty soon after that. George helped Michael clean up pieces of broken piñata as I pitched in to clear dirty cake plates with Mom and Nadia.

"I like George," Nadia whispered to Mom. "He's polite, mature, focused."

"I don't know," Mom said, louder than she should've. "I think he's a little stiff."

"Mom!" I cried, shushing her. "He'll hear you… and he's not stiff." I glanced at George, standing near Michael. Okay, the cashmere sweater and wingtips did make him look stiff. But he also seemed more relaxed out of his three-piece suit, though telling Mom he normally looked even stiffer would probably not win me any points. "I think the party and meeting my whole family at once was a little overwhelming."

That was probably why he said the weird things

about Jeremy cheating. He wanted to make a good impression but was nervous.

"You've got to give him credit for having the courage to show up at the zoo," Nadia added as she stacked dirty plates in the sink.

"That's something Peter would never have done," I reminded Mom. *And Robert might not have, either, not after his disappearing act. Not after he casually sauntered right out of my life.*

Then I remembered how he was at the kids' table at Dana's wedding. No, he probably would've nailed it.

If he'd shown up.

"Our little Cass is all grown up," Nadia whispered as she pretended fake tears of pride. "Going for the adult and not the noncommittal."

Well, I could've done without that reminder, but still, I appreciated Nadia going to bat for me against Mom.

"If you say so." Mom's disapproval felt like a damp blanket over everything. Couldn't she see George was better for me?

"Oh, come on, Mom," I pleaded. "Give him a chance. I'll tell you what. I'll invite him over for dinner and you can get to know him better."

Mom cocked her head to one side, and her expression told me she had no intention of getting to know him better. Then, she softened as if she'd changed her mind.

"Okay." She sighed. "That sounds…fair." At least she managed to sound neutral about it. That was probably as close to enthusiasm as I was going to get.

Eighteen

MOM AGREED TO COME TO my place for dinner the following Sunday, and when Friday rolled around, I decided to do a thorough cleaning of my condo from bathroom to hallway. Sometimes, my busy schedule meant I let the clutter build up, and I wasn't going to let some old magazines stand in the way of Mom getting to know George. I was convinced that if she could just spend a little more time with him, she'd start to like him. She'd see how safe, how... dependable he was.

I needed to convince Mom she ought to forget Robert. And I needed to convince myself to forget about him, too. He was out of the picture, done. Though that didn't stop me from thinking about him from time to time, wondering how he was doing or if he'd even given me a second thought.

I remembered his indifferent tone on the phone.

He hadn't texted or called since that conversation. *This just confirms the fact he was never serious about me.*

As I cleaned dishes, I felt a pool of water leak near my toes on the kitchen floor. I shut off the tap and then swung open the cabinet beneath my sink. Sure enough, a steady trickle poured from the pipe, dribbling down to the cabinet and running off onto my floor. Duke came over to inspect the floor, sniffing at the puddle.

"No, Duke," I told him. "That's not drinking water."

I frowned. I glanced at the clock and realized it might be too late to call a plumber. If I did, I'd be charged after-hour fees. Right then, my phone rang. George called me every day about this time, which I found comforting, and especially reassuring on a day like today.

"Hey, George." I cradled the phone between my shoulder and cheek, as I grabbed some tea towels to mop up the mess.

"What's wrong?" he asked immediately. Points to him for picking up the stress in my voice. That was considerate.

"My sink is leaking. And it's spreading all over the floor. I'll have to call a plumber and…"

"Wait," George said. "I'll be right over. Maybe I can fix it. Do you have a toolbox?"

I thought about Dad's old toolbox, the one I'd inherited when he died. Mom said I ought to have it, since she already had a whole shed in the backyard filled with Dad's other tools. Dad was one of the handiest people around, and he seemed to be forever tinkering with something in the workshop in the garage. Mom never used it, opting to call the neighborhood handyman whenever something needed fixing. She'd cleaned out most of the tools a few years ago to make room for more storage, and that was when she'd sent me home with Dad's red metal toolbox. I'd used it often. I was pretty sure whatever George needed would be in there.

"I do," I said.

"Then I'll be right over. Ten minutes tops."

George actually arrived in seven. He was wearing a three-piece suit, back to the vest, tie and jacket. He took off his suit coat and rolled up his white, crisply pressed sleeves. Duke, I noticed, steered clear of George, which wasn't like him. Normally, Duke bounded up to any guest, eager for a pat on the head. I guessed Duke remembered his awkward introduction to George, who clearly wasn't a dog person. I stared at Duke, and he studied me with his dark brown eyes. I imagined he was thinking, *Where's Robert? Why's this guy back?*

"George, I can't thank you enough for this," I said.

I glanced at his expensive suit. "Are you sure you don't mind getting that dirty?"

"Not at all," he said as he grabbed a wrench and got to work. He lay down on my kitchen floor and inspected the pipes. I wondered if the man even *owned* grub clothes. I'd never seen him wear anything that didn't look brand new.

"Is it bad?" I asked him, hoping he could manage to fix it. I was also impressed that he was lying on my floor, expensive vest and matching pants and all.

"Don't you worry," George said. "I see where it's coming from. I'll have it as good as new in no time."

He cranked the wrench a few more times. Water sprayed out suddenly from the pipe, splashing George right in the face. He yelped.

"Should I call a plumber?"

"No," he said, straining as he tightened the pipe. He swiped at his forehead with his sleeve. "I think I got it. Just give me a second."

He grunted once more as he strained to tighten the pipe. He let out a triumphant little yelp and pulled himself up to his feet. "There you go," he said as he wiped his hands on a tea towel.

"Thanks," I said, sincerely grateful. He'd probably just saved me from a five-hundred-dollar plumber's bill. "This is so nice of you," I went on, meaning it. "I don't know why I'm surprised because I should have expected it. You're so dependable, and I know I can really rely on you." *Unlike Robert, who disappears in the middle of the night.* "I love that."

"Well, thank you." George smiled at me. Were we sharing a moment? He took one step closer, and then I knew: we were definitely sharing a moment. Was he about to kiss me?

Duke let out a low growl. Nothing too mean, just a warning. *Back off my mom,* he seemed to be telling George. The message hit its intended target. George took a step back, looking uneasily at my dog.

"Duke," I warned him, wondering what had come over him. He'd never growled at anyone. Not once. "Behave."

"It's all right. He's just being protective," George said, thankfully not taking offense.

"The more time he spends with you, the more he'll warm up to you," I promised, even though I wasn't sure why Duke hadn't already warmed up to him. Duke was a people dog. He liked *everyone*—except, it seemed, George. I frowned at my golden retriever.

"I'm sure he will," George agreed, though he eyed my dog with some suspicion. "Well, sink problem fixed. Anything else?"

"If only you knew how to install snow tires." That was the next to-do on my list.

"Cassandra." George's eyes grew wide with concern.

"You really need to get that done by a professional." His tone made me think I was a little girl again and I'd just gotten in trouble for sneaking a cookie before dinner. "The Insurance Institute for Highway Safety recommends that radials are used all year round now."

"Interesting. Did they tell you this personally?" I teased.

"As a matter of fact, they did." He was dead serious. Oh, geez. They actually had.

"Um, right. I'll…uh, make sure I do that."

Saturday, I hit the tire shop, first thing. I didn't want George bringing it up over dinner with Mom on Sunday. If she found his obsession with piñata-hitting rules bothersome, I knew she'd go ballistic over him lecturing me about my car tires. Mom believed she'd raised independent daughters and didn't like to be told otherwise, and George's "I know best" attitude wouldn't be well received.

Sure, George could be…well, serious and a little too focused on the rules, but wasn't that a good thing for me? I'd let the tires slide for months, and winter was in full swing. This was Denver. It's not like we ever had a snow-free winter. George wanted to make sure I was safe, and maybe I needed someone to look after me.

The tire guy with the mustache and big grin was nice as he filled out my paperwork at the mechanic's office. Their sign above the register listed the usual suspects: muffler, tires, transmission—anything and everything. He looked at his computer, searching for my tires, and then clucked his tongue.

"Miss Brand," he said, shaking his head. "You're not going to believe this, but we ran out of rubber."

"What?" I didn't understand. They were a tire shop, right?

"Just kidding," the tire guy said, almost apologetically. "Little tire humor. But not funny."

No, it could've been funny. Geez...was George rubbing off on me? Had I lost my sense of humor?

I pushed the unkind thought away. Sure, George wasn't playful. He didn't crack jokes—or acknowledge them, actually—but he was reliable and dependable, and I was certain he'd never hurt me.

"We don't have your tires in stock, but we can get them here in a couple of hours. Would you be willing to wait?"

"Ahhh..."

A couple of hours seemed like a drag, but then again, so did listening to George tell me about his buddies at the Insurance Institute for Highway Safety.

"Coffee and a couch that way." The tire guy pointed down the hall. I glanced at the all-but-packed waiting room. It seemed I wasn't the only one who'd put off the snow tire switch.

"You know what? I'll go for a walk and come back," I said and headed toward the door and the frigid winter air.

Outside, the majestic Rocky Mountains sprang up beside the small tire dealer, and I glanced up at their snowcapped peaks. They never ceased to amaze me. I felt so lucky to live in a place so gorgeous. Then I looked around and saw...Robert.

Ack!

He stood less than three feet from me, hanging a poster promoting a Lantern Festival across one of the shop's glass windows. He looked so good—brown hair perfectly swept back, broad shoulders as wide as I remembered, dark eyes fixed on his project. He'd notice me any second as he seemed about to secure the last bit of tape on the edge of the poster. I scooted by him, head down, using my smartphone as a little shield. It didn't work.

"No, no, no," he called after me, shoving his hands deep into his pockets, his breath coming out in white puffs. "If you want to hide from me, you're going to have to run faster than that."

I froze, cringed, and turned. Nothing about this was awkward at all, was it? I loved running into handsome men who'd deserted me in the wee hours of the morning. Charming men I dated and then dumped.

"Robert," I said, trying to act like I hadn't noticed him when obviously I had. "What are you doing here?"

A sly smile crept onto Robert's face. He didn't seem angry to see me. *Odd.*

"Hi," he said, and I felt my insides go warm and gooey. Those eyes…I'd forgotten their effect on me. "Getting my transmission worked on. You?"

"Tires," I murmured, shifting awkwardly from one foot to the other. A biting chill laced the air, but I barely felt it—not while Robert looked at me.

"Ah." Robert rocked back on his heels. "So, here we wait…*together.*" He put a lot of emphasis on that last word.

"Mmm-hmmm." I pressed my lips together. Would I be waiting here *with Robert* for two hours? This might have gone from awkward to unbearable. *Ugh.* I felt like a jerk for ending it with him like I did, but then again, hadn't he skipped out on me that morning?

"So, our last date…"

Oh, no. Here we go with the post-relationship analysis. Panic rose in my throat. The only thing I hated more than talking about feelings was talking about *relationships.*

"…was bad," Robert finished.

"Maybe," I agreed, thinking more about Robert sneaking out and less about the ambulance ride.

"It was bad, but you know what? It wasn't my worst date ever," he said. "I once went on a date with a woman who had a warrant out for her arrest. I kid you not. Sheriff's deputies took her right before dessert."

"Oh, I can top that." I fell into conversation with Robert as if we'd never broken up. "I had a blind date with an older guy. Turned out, he was *thirty* years older. He fell asleep at dinner, and I had to save him from drowning in his mashed potatoes."

Robert laughed, and so did I. Goodness, I loved his laugh, deep and rich, like I imagine chocolate might sound. I missed this. I missed the banter, and, frankly, I missed *laughing*. I didn't do that a lot with George.

"That's bad," Robert agreed. "But at least you didn't have to go to the emergency room."

"Oh, I didn't mind that," I said. "Gotta put my health insurance to use, or why have it?"

Robert grinned.

"But...I thought maybe you hated that date more than me," I said, unable to stop myself. "Since you left without saying good-bye."

Robert blanched. "I left a note."

What? "You did?"

"Right on your coffee table, near the side with Duke's bed..."

I froze as I realized what had probably happened. Duke had gotten up sometime in the early morning and knocked off the note. Maybe he'd even eaten it. My dog did like to chew things. Or, more likely, I'd find it under my couch.

Ugh. I was such an idiot.

"So you didn't sneak out?" Robert hadn't hurt me on purpose. He hadn't intended on hurting me at all. *Robert had never snuck out. He'd left a note.*

"No!" Robert shook his head hard, brown hair flopping. "I had to go let Daisy out, and the poor dog was doing a potty dance when I got home. I left a note asking you to call, and saying I was sorry for barging into your house and babysitting you, and that I'd let you make the next move. But you didn't." Robert rubbed his neck sheepishly. "I guess that's because you never got the note."

Suddenly, I felt like garbage. The reason he hadn't texted for two days was because he was giving me space...because he thought I might be mad he'd insisted on staying overnight. Robert *had* cared. I could tell by the way he looked at me now. I realized it hadn't just been about having a note or not having it. I'd kicked Robert to the curb because I'd wanted Dr. Susie to be right. The whirlwind of emotions Robert dredged up scared me.

"I'm sorry things ended the way they did," I said,

hoping he believed me. "And to be honest, it's nothing you did. It's me."

"Really?" Robert raised his eyebrows, looking skeptical. *It's not you, it's me.*

"I know how that sounds," I said. "But it's true. See…I always go for the same type of guy…a guy like you. Funny, handsome, charming." I thought of all that Robert had in common with my exes. "And it never works out."

Usually because they bolted—or I did—before things got too serious. Actually, thinking about it, I'd done most of the bolting. In fact, I think I'd broken up with ninety percent of those guys. Maybe Dr. Susie was right: *I* was the commitment-phobe.

I said, "I just need to start making better decisions in that department."

Robert cocked his head to one side. "So, instead of giving me a chance, you decided to sabotage any possibility at a relationship."

Wow, when he put it like that, I sounded like a real jerk. But he wasn't wrong.

"Yep, pretty much." I sighed. "I'm just…" Now probably wouldn't be the time to tell him that I'd turned over all life choices to Dr. Susie. "I'm trying to change the way I choose relationships, and you just happened to get caught up in the middle of that. So, I'm sorry."

"Okay," Robert said, nodding and looking at his shoes. "Well, thank you for your honesty."

"Yeah." I still felt like a jerk, though.

"Okay, so we can both stand here, waiting, probably endlessly," Robert said, another sly smile tugging at the corners of his mouth. "Or...there's a bowling alley up the street. We could go bowl away our boredom."

I thought about George. I thought about dinner tomorrow with Mom. I also thought about how much I wanted to go. But...*I shouldn't*. What's done was done.

"Oh, I don't know if that's a good idea." Actually, I did know for sure: it was a terrible idea. I could feel the electric current of attraction snapping between us. I *still* wondered what it would be like to kiss Robert. And wasn't I dating George now? I mean, we technically hadn't had the "we're exclusive" talk yet, but I'd specifically broken things off with Robert so I could focus on George. Bowling with Robert didn't seem likely to help me do that.

"Okay," Robert said, nodding and shrugging one shoulder. "Well, I'm gonna go, but you can stay right here. I mean, this parking lot looks like a lot of fun. And that..." He gestured to the near-to-bursting waiting room with a crying toddler pushing his button nose against the glass window. "That looks like fun, too."

Well, he had a point there. I didn't want to wait in the cold *or* in the crowded waiting room.

"Fine, I'll go," I said. "But *only* as a friend."

"Okay, friends it is," Robert agreed.

The bowling alley sat less than a block from the dealership. We walked in, and instantly, I knew I'd have a blast. REO Speedwagon blared from the speakers, and it almost felt like fate had a hand in this place.

"You've got to pay your way now," Robert said. "You're in the friend zone."

I laughed a little. I'd forgotten what a good sport Robert was and how he never let anything get him down for long. Just like Dad. Dad probably would've adored Robert if he'd lived to meet him. He would've been an even bigger fan than Mom. Of this, I had no doubt.

We began our game, and when a waiter bustled by, Robert ordered French fries. "Want anything?" he asked me.

"No," I said. The menu was a nutritionist's disaster: French fries, cheese sticks, and hot dogs. Nothing came with a single fruit or vegetable, unless you counted ketchup.

I rolled the ball and hit all the pins but one. As I

set up for a second turn, tucking the yellow ball to my chin, Robert booed, trying to distract me.

"Quiet," I admonished. "I want to hear a pin drop."

"Pfft." Robert rolled his eyes. "Spare me."

Unfazed, I reared back and let the bowling ball fly. It rolled down the lane and smacked right into the last remaining pin. That was how to pull out a spare.

"Nice shot," Robert admitted.

"Thanks. Well, I *was* sixth grade bowling champion. I've got a trophy to prove it." Dad had been so proud of me that day. Bowling was his game.

The waiter returned with a piping hot basket of French fries. The smell hit my nose and my stomach protested. It might not be chocolate cake, but I was hungry. I sat next to Robert and reached over to grab a fry, but he playfully bobbed and weaved, keeping the basket away from me.

"Oh, no, no, no. I don't share my food with 'friends.'"

Touché. "Well...fine. Be a French fry hog."

"You can call me what you want," Robert declared. "I am not sharing my food anymore."

He sounded playful, but maybe sharing food *had* meant something to him. Maybe it wasn't as easy for him to share as I'd thought. Maybe he was more like me, territorial with his food, but he'd liked me so much he'd given in.

I glanced at the scoreboard on the screen above our heads. "It's your turn," I pointed out. "What are you going to do about your fries?"

"Watch." Robert sprang up, holding the basket in one hand, and grabbed his bowling ball with the other. He wasn't really going to bowl like that, was he?

"Really?" I challenged.

"Really." He let the ball fly, but it rattled into the gutter.

"Oh! Gutter ball." I gave him a slow, sarcastic clap. "Oh, that's a shame. But you know what? I'll give you a do-over for some fries."

"Nope." Robert wasn't budging. "I'm going to keep my gutter ball and keep my tasty fries." He popped one into his mouth to rub it in.

But I wasn't giving up on those fries. My stomach growled. It demanded one, even as he rolled his second ball, which only knocked down two pins.

"How about we share the fries and..." I tried to think of an angle. "And the loser pays for them?"

Robert barked a laugh. "Why do I feel like I'm being hustled?"

Because he was. My sixth-grade bowling trophy was no fluke. "Do we have a deal?"

"Uh, sure. Okay. It's your turn." Robert moved back so I could grab my ball. Victory was mine.

"This is where I get my revenge," I declared,

picking up my trusty yellow ball. Robert set down his fries and then jumped in front of me as if to block me.

"What are you doing?" I couldn't help but giggle. He looked ridiculous, waving his arms as if he planned to deflect a basketball.

"Playing defense," Robert declared.

"But we're *bowling.*"

"Yeah? There's a whole basket of tasty fries at stake."

"Yeah, but I'm holding a bowling ball," I said. "I could hurt you." Like, seriously. I tried to imagine George doing something so reckless and couldn't. He'd probably lecture me on the dangers of bowling injuries and opt to take me to the opera instead.

"If you bowl like you putt, I think I'm safe. I'll take my chances." Robert continued to bob back and forth in front of me. He went right and then left, arms outstretched, and I found no way to get around him. So, I ducked and rolled the ball straight between his legs. We both watched as the ball made its way precariously down the lane...and knocked over all the pins. Strike!

I jumped up and shouted. "Yesss!" I punched Robert on the shoulder. "This is why cheating will never get you anywhere in life."

Oh, geez. Did a George quote just pop out of my mouth?

Robert looked as surprised as I felt. One eyebrow rose on his face as if to say, *Since when do you care about the rules?* "I can't believe you just said that."

Neither could I. Was I becoming like George? Even if he was rubbing off on me, shouldn't that make me glad? Instead, it made me uneasy.

"You're up," I said quickly, hoping to gloss over the fact I'd just taken on the role of "Stickler for the Rules" when Robert clearly never gave rules a second thought—except how to creatively break them. "Are you ready?"

I took my spot playing defense. It was my turn to mess with *his* shot. I wasn't George, and I'd prove it.

"Come on," I dared him.

He tucked his ball under his chin and grinned. He grabbed me with one arm and pulled me into a half hug as he let his ball fly. I'd forgotten how tall—how broad—Robert was. He pulled me into his body as if I was a little kid. The ball, however, hit the gutter again and rolled harmlessly into the back without connecting with a single pin, though he didn't look like he much cared.

"This is why you should never cheat," I managed to say softly, struggling against his arm but failing. He had me in a tight grip. I wasn't going anywhere. He wrapped his other hand around to keep me in place. He felt so warm and strong, and I liked how close we were. He smelled good, too. Like cinnamon and something sweet. I stopped struggling and he moved back from me so we were face-to-face. Oh, boy. Those eyes. And his full lips. I'd never kissed him, and I wanted to know what that was like.

He came closer and I let him. I wanted this.

He laid his lips on mine, and a current ran straight to my toes. Oh, he was a talented kisser, just like I'd knew he'd be. He put his big hands on the small of my back and pulled me into him as he deepened the kiss. Soft, insistent, but with a simmering heat that surprised me. The rest of the bowling alley melted away, and suddenly, all that mattered was Robert—his lips on mine, his hands on my waist. My whole brain lit up in a series of exploding fireworks. How long did we kiss? Two seconds? An hour? Time seemed to shift and no longer mattered. All that mattered was being in Robert's arms. I never wanted it to stop.

I could do this forever. Would do this forever, except...*George*.

Dr. Susie had picked George, not Robert. I was backsliding into my old ways. I had to remain strong.

My eyes flew open and I pulled away. I saw Robert panting and realized I was too. So, he'd felt the fireworks as well.

"I'm sorry. I-I can't." It wasn't fair to George.

Robert wiped his bottom lip. "You sure?"

No, I wasn't sure at all. Every fiber in my being wanted to stay right here with Robert and kiss him again. But I couldn't. I scrambled away from him and grabbed my coat and purse, suddenly lightheaded. Was that from the kiss?

"Thank you for the game," I blurted, even as I saw Robert looking confused, standing at the edge of the lane. He let me go. He didn't try to stop me. I took one last look at him as I traded my bowling shoes in for my snow boots. His dark eyes never left me as I headed for the door.

Nineteen

I COULDN'T STOP THINKING ABOUT ROBERT and the toes-on-fire kiss we'd shared. I could feel the electricity run straight through my toes. Meanwhile, George hadn't even *tried* to kiss me, so I had no idea what that would be like. And Mom was coming over for dinner tonight, when my only job would be to try to convince her George was a suitable boyfriend. If I told her about Robert and the stolen kiss, she'd flip. She'd tell me all those sparks meant I should be with Robert. I knew how she felt about sparks, and we had no shortage of those.

I worked on creating my signature chicken and sundried tomato pasta—my mom's recipe—as well as a kale salad. Mom arrived early and in a good mood. She hugged me and sniffed the air.

"Ooh, I smell chicken and sundried tomatoes," she sang as she moved into the kitchen and immediately inspected the skillet on the stove. Duke galloped up to her, tail wagging enthusiastically. She gave him a generous scratch behind the ears.

"You bet it is," I said.

"So, give me the vitals on George," she said, glancing at me. "What does he do for a living again?"

"Well… He…" I paused. "He's in insurance." He ran an insurance company, yes, but there was more to it than that, wasn't there? I remembered him talking about his day-to-day office duties, but when I tried to explain them, I couldn't.

Thankfully, the doorbell rang, saving me. I buzzed George up to my condo, and he arrived wearing a wool coat and a suit, which seemed a tad too formal, and when he leaned in and gave me a cool peck on the cheek, I couldn't help but compare his lukewarm affection to Robert's sizzling heat when he'd pressed his lips to mine. I mentally shook myself. *No thinking of Robert. Time to focus on George.*

George carried several white bakery boxes. Duke sat down, glaring at George. I was almost glad he hadn't seen how happy my dog was to see my mother. He wouldn't be able to help but draw a comparison.

"What are those?" I asked as he set them gently on my granite countertops.

"A surprise," he said and shrugged out of his winter coat. "Mrs. Brand," George said. Mom went in for a hug, but George oddly stuck out his hand for a shake. She took it, awkwardly. Duke growled a little, wary.

"Duke," I admonished. He looked up at me, his expression saying, *Really? This guy again?* Then he trotted over to his doggy bed and lay down, head on his paws in defeat.

"Hi, George," she said, tone unimpressed.

Ugh. We were off to a rocky start.

"Anybody hungry?" I chimed in quickly as I rustled up some dinner plates from my cabinet.

"Starved," George said. He took his seat at the head of my dining table. Mom's eyebrows raised ever so slightly, and she glanced at me. I knew without her saying a word, she was thinking, *He expects to be served?* But I also knew George was simply trying to be a good dinner guest and stay out of the kitchen. Still, I could see how it looked.

"I'll get the plates, Mom. You go ahead and have a seat." I smiled at her and ushered her to a chair. I piled on pasta for each of them and then brought the huge bowl of salad to the table. We settled in, and conversation turned to benign topics: the recent snowfall, the highway construction near Mom's house, and whether the Avalanche hockey team would make it to the playoffs in April. Duke never begged at the table, and he stayed resolutely in his dog bed, watching us. I inhaled my food, in part because I was nervous, and in part because I was eager to find out what might be in those bakery boxes.

"Time for that surprise, I think." I looked at George.

"Surprise?" Mom asked, curiosity piqued.

"By all means." George patted his lips stiffly with his napkin, but made no move to serve the desserts, so I got up. Mom, sensing chocolate in the vicinity, joined me. We opened the bakery boxes to find a tantalizing collection of delectable sweets: profiteroles, éclairs, and tarts. I sucked in a breath. Mom perked up suddenly. Finally, George had won points!

"These desserts are beautiful, George," I said, as I gently moved each one to separate plates. Mom and I took them to the table.

"Dinner was so delicious, I thought bringing desserts from my favorite patisserie was the least I could do."

He let his French accent weigh heavily on *patisserie* and I glanced at Mom to see her frown ever so slightly.

"So…" I needed to change the subject fast, before Mom cracked a joke or asked *what the heck is a patisserie?* "Before you arrived, I was trying to explain to Mom what you do for a living, but I thought you could explain better."

"Well, I can try." George turned to my mother, who attempted to keep her attention on George, even as one eye seemed to be focused on a berry tart in front of her. "I own a company, an insurance service. We investigate automobile accidents and then help determine liability and provide cost analysis."

Mom helped herself to a profiterole and a tart.

"Oh," she exclaimed. "That sounds exciting, going out and investigating like a detective—" Mom, to her credit, really tried to make his job sound exciting. But before she could get too far along in her analogy, George cut her off.

"No," he said, shaking his head. "No, we don't go out and investigate. I manage the people who review the facts surrounding the accident."

Mom frowned slightly, confused. "So, *they're* the detectives?"

"Not really." George would *not* let Mom have this one. *Argh.* Why wouldn't he just let her believe he was Sherlock Holmes? Who cared if that wasn't exactly the truth of his job? Robert would've let Mom run with her detective analogy, let her have her fun. There was Robert again. I needed to *stop* thinking of him and that kiss.

To distract myself from *that* uncomfortable thought, I stared at George's dessert. He'd grabbed a profiterole—the last perfect one. The one left on the platter in the middle of the table had a broken end. I glanced down at the tart on my plate and suddenly felt the pang of dessert envy.

"As a team, we go over the evidence, talk to witnesses, get statements from drivers," George droned on, "and then I spend hours calculating loss ratios and negotiating, trying to save the company money."

I reached over with my fork to grab a bite off George's plate, but he blocked me with his own fork. The tines of his fork and mine clanked together.

"I actually brought enough for each of us to have one," George said.

I let my fork hang there in the air, entangled with George's. He'd blocked me from his dessert, and he was serious about it. I recovered, aware that Mom was watching—and judging—every move. "Of course," I said, retreating quickly and taking a gulp of wine. I bit my lip, not making eye contact with Mom. I didn't know whether or not I felt more embarrassed for George for coming off as stingy or me for coming off as a glutton. Either way, my face felt like it was on fire.

"Gloria," George began, taking a bite of his dessert. "What do you do for fun?"

"Oh, well." My mom thankfully did not address the awkward fork-fighting incident. "For one, I like playing on my iPad. I just discovered Facebook."

I held my breath. Was she going to talk about being friends with Robert?

George said, "Oh, that's one of those time killers I've never been interested in."

Mom set her mouth in a thin line and steepled her hands beneath her chin. Her expression couldn't be clearer as she glanced at me: *who is this stick in the mud?* I nudged George under the table.

"But of course, if you enjoy it, then by all means, you should continue." George fumbled awkwardly for a save. By the look on Mom's face, he'd failed. She obviously did not need his permission to do anything. I sucked in a breath. This dinner was a disaster. A Category Five. Someone call FEMA.

"So…" Mom cleared her throat. "I know how you two met, but what do *you* do for fun?" There seemed to be a slight edge to Mom's tone—as if she were skeptical we could even *have* fun. I was eager to prove her wrong.

"Well, George and I are both adventurous," I said. I knew Mom would like that word. She always used it to describe Dad. "We like to discover new music and fine dining…and art."

Mom's knuckles grew a little white as she clasped her hands tighter beneath her chin. She seemed to be trying very hard to censor whatever she was thinking.

"Really?" Mom raised a single, doubtful eyebrow. "I didn't know you liked art."

"Oh, I do," I managed quickly, though my voice

sounded high and strained, even to my own ears. But I was a sophisticated, educated woman, wasn't I? I could like art. "And going to a gallery. Like George said, that's an adventure."

Mom narrowed her eyes a bit but only murmured a suspicious, "Umm-hmm." I was beginning to think this evening had been a huge mistake. Mom spending time with George only seemed to make her like him less. And if she felt this way about George, I wondered what Dad would've thought if he were here.

The rest of dessert, thankfully, sped by in harmless small talk, but I could sense there was nothing harmless in Mom's quickly darkening mood. I tried to save the evening by explaining how George had saved me from a huge plumbing bill by fixing my leaky sink, but Mom just nodded her head and smiled weakly. Even George's show of chivalry didn't faze her.

George mentioned an early-morning client meeting the next day, and I didn't try to persuade him to stay. He got his coat, and Mom and I walked him to the door.

"You have raised an amazing daughter," George told Mom.

She smiled tightly. "Thank you," she said. "I know."

He seemed a little surprised, and I almost thought he might chastise her for bragging. *Please, don't*, I silently hoped. He didn't, thankfully. "I'll call you tomorrow," he told me. And I knew he would, right at seven sharp, like he always did. Then he leaned in and gave me another cold peck on the cheek. I didn't expect him to try to kiss me with Mom here, but at the same time...the kiss on the cheek felt barren of all emotion, like a European greeting between two near-strangers. "Thanks for a wonderful evening." He walked out the open door.

"Good night," I called and then shut the door behind him. I swallowed, turning to face the firing squad of Mom. *Might as well get this over with.* I knew it would be bad. The question was: how bad?

"So...second impression?" I braced myself for her answer.

"Well..." Mom inhaled as she clearly tried to think of something nice to say. "His work seems important and...useful."

Oh, boy. *Useful?* That was the best thing she could say? This was going to be worse than I thought.

"And he is quite polite," she said, still reaching for something positive to say. "Good manners and..." She ran out of nice things to tell me.

I crossed my arms. "And you don't like him."

Mom exhaled. "No, I don't really." She shrugged, looking uncomfortable. "But I just don't understand why you like him."

I felt defensive suddenly. "Lots of reasons," I said and then found myself scrambling to name one. "He's dependable. Reliable. Well-put-together." Almost too put-together, if I counted the number of vests in the man's closet.

Mom shook her head at me slowly. "Those are all great words for a major appliance, but not ones you should use to describe your boyfriend." She leaned against my dining room table. "What about 'fun' or 'exciting'?"

"Right." I held up my hand like a school crossing guard. "But we know I'm trying to grow *away* from being attracted to that kind of guy, right?"

Mom clutched the back of one of my dining room chairs and sighed. "Again with that…book." She very nearly spat out the word.

"I am trying to find a man who will commit to a mature relationship, and you know what? That could be George."

"Yeah, honey." Mom appeared so downtrodden. "Look, I don't know anything about anything in this modern world, but I listen to you and Nadia when you talk about what Dr. Susie promotes. And one of the things she asks is, if I remember correctly, 'Is he genuine? Or is he just acting differently to win you over?'"

I had no idea where Mom was going with this.

George was one of the most honest, upright people I knew—to a fault, really. "You don't think he's being genuine?"

Mom shook her head slowly. "Oh, no. *He's* definitely being genuine," she said. "The question is: are you?"

Twenty

I SPENT THE NEXT WEEK WONDERING if Mom was right. Was *I* being the fake one? Sure, I'd never listened to classical music *or* attended art galleries before I met George, but I liked those things, didn't I?

Or did I just *like the idea of liking them?* Or, worse, was I pretending to like them because I didn't want George to find me lacking? Sure, I could be a sophisticated woman of worldly tastes, but was that who I *wanted* to be? And maybe I had been in professional mode and hadn't let George see the real me—the carefree, playful Cass who liked bowling and blaring REO Speedwagon. Had I even *told* George they were my favorite band? Did George only like the professional, buttoned-up Cass?

Well, I figured there was one way to find out. It was time for *me* to pick our next date. No art galleries. No five-star restaurants. Corn dogs and putt-putt.

I decided to surprise George. I picked him up and drove, and I blared REO Speedwagon. He didn't comment on the choice of music or ask me about it.

"That's a little loud, isn't it?" he said, as he leaned over and turned down the volume. "Do I get a clue where we're going?"

I glanced at him, deciding to let the music go. "It's a surprise," I said, noticing that George wore a sweater and tie, though I'd definitely told him to go casual. When had casual ever included a tie? I was beginning to think I'd never see the man's collarbone. He always had his neck covered. George frowned and shifted awkwardly in his seat as I drove him into the putt-putt parking lot. He glanced up at the sign, skeptical.

"Isn't this for kids?" he asked me.

"Aren't we all kids at heart? Come on, it'll be fun." I parked the car and hopped out, taking George by the hand. After we'd gotten our putters and golf balls, we started on the course. We approached the infamous T. Rex hole, and George, oblivious to traps, stepped right in front of the T. Rex, who came to life with a loud, cackling roar. George jumped a mile, putting his hand over his heart.

"Don't worry." I laughed. "He's a herbivore. He only eats trees, bushes, and golf balls. You never know when a dinosaur will ruin your game—"

But George wasn't in the mood for jokes. His

mouth dipped down into a disapproving frown. "I never understood the need to shrink a fun sport and then add windmills, clown faces or…" He glared at the robot T. Rex. "…dinosaurs." He shook his head. "I also didn't realize how hot it was going to be." He tugged at his collar. The indoor course did have the heat cranked up. Then again, I'd told him to come casual. "But…if *this* is what you want to do…"

He clearly didn't approve as he dropped his ball on the Astroturf.

"I just thought it would be fun to loosen up… Be *ourselves*."

"I'll try anything…*once*," George said, implying he would likely never be back to this putt-putt course, despite not hitting one shot yet. He got ready to putt, staring intently at the ball. "As long as it's with you."

Aw, that was sweet! Sure, George could be stiff. But he was earnest. Honest. Loyal. There were a few more words that maybe Mom would approve of.

George tapped the ball a little too hard and it went past the hole. "Ugh," he sighed, exasperated.

"No, that was good. Really good!" I tried, but George just shook his head, too somber and annoyed he'd missed. Who took mini golf this seriously? It was a game. I suspected this little date of ours was going to be a long night. I had to try to loosen him up. Surely, George undid his Windsor knot *sometimes*.

George took another swing, but before it went too far, I jumped in the way of the ball.

"What are you doing?" George looked shocked, his face flushed with... Was that anger?

"Just playing a little defense." I tried to lighten the mood but quickly realized George was having none of it.

"In golf!" George looked like he might have a fit right there.

"*Miniature* golf," I corrected him. It was my turn, and I hit my ball straight to the hole. It sank in immediately. I pumped my fist in the air. "And that's how it's done!" I laughed, but George looked exasperated.

"George," I said, feeling bad all of a sudden. "If you're not enjoying this, I bet there are some games upstairs you might like."

George shook his head. "Cassandra, you are amazing. You are one of the most interesting, talented, and driven women I've ever met. And if you like this"—he glanced around uneasily—"this type of place, then I will learn to like it, too."

Aw, that was so nice! George was trying so hard. We stared at each other a beat. *Now would be a perfect time to make a move. Kiss me, already,* I wanted to scream but didn't. George just studied me, not moving. He arched his eyebrows slightly, and I knew he wasn't going to make the first move. I was tired of waiting. I needed to finally figure out whether or not we had any sparks. Impulsively, I reached up on my tiptoes, grabbed George by the neck, and planted a kiss on him.

He froze, not moving at all for a second.

For a heart-stopping, horrifying minute, I thought I was kissing a mannequin. Then he wiggled his lips ever so slightly. Barely. But I felt nothing, not a single spark. On the Richter Scale, that kiss landed as a flat zero.

George pulled himself away, looking flushed and embarrassed. "Wow, not exactly…private." Uneasily, he glanced around us, even though we were the only ones for at least two holes. "I didn't know you could be so…"

"Spontaneous? Passionate? Outgoing?" I offered, realizing Mom had been *so* right. I had been hiding part of myself this whole time. Trying to play dress-up, pretending I was someone refined and sophisticated and…buttoned-up. I was none of those things. "No, I don't think you've gotten to know any of those things about me since we started dating."

"I guess I haven't," he said softly.

"Or that I'm competitive or that I share food or…" I was starting to get upset. Tears burned the back of my eyes and my throat felt tight.

"Hey," he said, putting his hand on my elbow and squeezing. Even that gesture felt a little…cold. A bit too reserved. "We're just getting to know each other. I'm sure I will like all of these sides of you. I know I will, because I'm…falling…"

Oh, no. Not the L-word. No, not possible.

"No! George, you can't be falling in—whatever—with me because the truth is, you don't really know me." And I was certain, no matter what he said, he wouldn't like the *real* Cass. "I haven't been…genuine with you." Like, for instance, I never really wanted to go see an art gallery opening again. Or listen to any more classic music, or order from a menu where I didn't recognize *one* edible dish. "I mean, I let you call me Cassandra, but no one calls me by my full name." Only George and telemarketers.

"They don't?" He looked baffled, despite having heard every one of my family members calling me *Cass.*

"No, they don't." I shook my head slowly. Sadness hit me like a wall. George wasn't the one. Dr. Susie had been wrong.

"You are a great guy, and I've had a great time with you." I inhaled. "But I was spending so much time seeing if you could live up to some crazy standard that I haven't been myself with you. But I can't keep this act up for the rest of my life. At some point, you're going to realize I'm not the person you think I am."

My voice wobbled. Geez, I was going to cry! "I'm really sorry."

I sniffed hard, willing myself not to get so emotional, even as the first tear dribbled out.

"I don't know what to say," George managed after a beat.

"I know. I'm sorry." I looked upward, hoping the tears would roll back in their tear ducts. "Maybe I should just drive you home?"

He swallowed, looking at his feet. "Yeah, I guess you should."

After the most awkward good-bye on the planet, I dropped George off and went back to my condo feeling sad, yet relieved. He was not the right man for me and I knew it. I'd known it for a long time. As much as I hated that Mom was right, I had to admit she'd nailed it. I'd been so intent on trying to follow Dr. Susie's rules, so desperate for them to work, I'd somehow lost *the real me.*

I thought about Robert again, the feel of his lips on mine. I'd always been comfortably myself with him. Yet…it was too late for us, wasn't it? Besides, he'd failed all of Dr. Susie's tests, and even though she'd been wrong about George, was I ready to abandon her philosophy altogether? If I did, how was I ever supposed to find a mature man for a grown-up relationship? Dr. Susie had successfully gutted my confidence in my own instincts.

I took a deep breath. So, George was the wrong guy. I could just take my Dr. Susie list on to the next one, right? I could keep looking.

The next morning, I took Duke for a run during a surprisingly warm winter's day. Snow still dotted the ground, but most of the recent snowfall had melted, and we managed to avoid the icy spots, enjoying the unseasonably mild afternoon. The ice-capped Rockies stood majestically before us as we ran, Duke's tongue lolling out, me trying to live in the moment. When we returned to my condo, I felt renewed, lungs full of fresh mountain air. I clicked on *Wake Up Denver,* noticing that Dr. Susie would be on next.

What a coincidence. She had a new book. I turned up the sound. Maybe *this* book would be the answer to all my problems.

Kyle, one of the two show hosts, said, "Before we get to Dr. Susie, if you're looking for something fun to do tonight, Cissy and I will be hosting the Lantern Festival." A poster appeared onscreen that looked familiar. Then I remembered—it was the poster Robert had been hanging up at the tire shop when I'd run into him. This was one of *his* events!

I recalled our kiss once more...and the look of

total heartbreak on his face when I'd scooted out of that bowling alley.

Robert had texted me once, telling me he was sorry if he'd overstepped. I told him not to worry—it was me, not him. I hadn't heard from him over the last week, but could I blame him? How many ways could I say no?

"Okay, to kick things off today," Cissy, the morning co-host, said, "we are once again talking to one of our favorite writers, Dr. Susie, author of her just-released book, *Dissecting Divorce—how to leave your not-so-perfect mate behind.*"

Wait...what? Dr. Susie wrote a book on *divorce*?

"After the success of several self-help and relationship bestsellers, Dr. Susie is now helping those who have loved and lost," Kyle said.

Honestly, was this for real? Dr. Susie and divorce? I scoffed as I grabbed an orange from my fruit bowl. This ought to be interesting. Dr. Susie looked like her professional self, and yet...I had to admit, she seemed a little tired and run-down. Not quite as perfectly put together as usual.

"As you know, Kyle, I am in the midst of what's becoming a very public divorce," Dr. Susie began. I nearly spit out my orange. Divorce? The perfect Dr. Susie? "And, ladies, after a breakup, you are going to have moments of doubt, and you'll want to blame yourself for this loss." Dr. Susie stared at the camera, and it felt once more as if she might be talking directly to me. "But, let me tell you: it's not you. It's the man!"

I barked a laugh out loud. Seriously? She'd been saying it was *us* for years. I even *believed* her, and now she was reversing her whole philosophy on men?

I wanted to slap myself. This is the woman I'd been thinking was an infallible guru? The woman I'd let throw a grenade into my dating life and make me doubt myself and my own instincts? *Ugh.* I should *never* have listened to Nadia in the first place. And I should've *always* listened to my gut. After all, it had told me George was no match for me.

Had I blown it with Robert when maybe *he* was the one I was truly meant to be with? Mom sure thought so. I had to admit, so did I. I'd let Dr. Susie and *The Dater's Handbook* get in my head and ruin everything. Mom had been right all along. That book was nonsense.

When I got to work that morning, I was still fuming about Dr. Susie and her about-face. When I opened my drawer, looking for a client file, and saw that awful *Handbook,* I grabbed it and slung it into the trash, nearly hitting Dana on her way into my office with my coffee.

"Whoa," she murmured, stopping in her tracks as she set the coffee down on my desk. She glanced at that wastepaper basket. "*The Dater's Handbook*? You? Really?"

I let out a long, defeated sigh. "I don't know why you're surprised," I said. "We all know my dating history, and I figured if it worked for you and Jim, maybe I'd give it a try."

Dana's face wrinkled in confusion. "Wait…you think Jim and I…?" She pulled the *Handbook* out of the trash and held it up with disdain. "Please."

"But I saw it in your desk."

"It was a *gag* gift from my cousin," Dana explained. "Dr. Susie would never approve of my relationship. Jim is crazy. I never know what he's going to say or do next. Or if he's even going to show up on time. It's always a puzzle, but I'm never bored." Love for Jim shone in her voice. "He's the most interesting person I know. He keeps me on my toes. All the time."

I found myself instantly thinking of Robert. He sure kept me on my toes all the time. He *was* a puzzle, a handsome, sparks-inducing puzzle, and I had to admit, when I was with him, I was never bored.

"And you know what? Who wants someone boring, anyway?" Dana tossed the book into the trash and left my office.

She was so right. But was it too late to mend things with Robert? I'd been awful to him. I'd dumped him twice, pretty much.

As if fate were intervening, Nadia called.

"Want to join us at the Lantern Festival tonight? Jeremy is so excited and Mom's coming, too."

I bit my fingernail. Would Robert be there? I felt excitement tickle my belly. Maybe I could apologize. Beg for forgiveness?

"Uh, yes, sure," I said before I could change my mind. "That sounds like fun. I'd love to."

"Great. Well, we'll pick you up at six."

"Okay, see you soon," I said and ended the call.

I had to figure out what I was going to wear, and what I would say to Robert if I happened to see him. And I really, really hoped I'd see him.

Twenty-one

A<small>N HOUR INTO THE PACKED</small> street festival, I began to curse Fate. She seemed to be a rotten planner, because while I'd seen a dozen colorful Chinese dragon dancers and the ever-present thump of drums, I'd not seen a sign of Robert the whole night. Hundreds of people lined the streets in downtown Denver, and I was beginning to think my whole plan of "accidentally" bumping into Robert and then apologizing until I was blue in the face would never materialize. *Ugh.* Where was he? I glanced through the crowd, not seeing him.

Nadia walked beside me, and Jeremy held Michael's hand ahead of us as he pointed at a bright red dragon dancing its way down the street.

"What a wonderful turnout," Cissy, the Denver morning show host said, her voice booming across several amplifiers.

I wish there were fewer people. Maybe then I could find Robert.

"If you haven't already," her co-host, Kyle, announced into his microphone, "get your lanterns. We'll be launching them in about ten minutes."

I looked at a few volunteers, handing out white lanterns. None of them were Robert. Michael took several and gave one to my nephew. Jeremy grabbed his lantern and his candle, eager for the big lighting ceremony when the lanterns would fill the Denver skyline. The pleasant sounds of a bamboo flute carried across the wind. Nadia had been trying to convince me that Dr. Susie's advice was sound, even if it eventually led to her own divorce. Mom clearly thought I was absolutely right in ditching Dr. Susie but kept silent as Nadia tried to convince me I should give the talk show therapist another chance.

"I really think we should go back to the start," she said. "Chapter One: It's Not the Man, It's You."

"No," I said, laughing a little. I hadn't yet told Nadia her self-help guru was a fraud, but I figured she'd find out in due time. "I think I'll just do it on my own now." I scanned the crowd. Robert had to be here.

Nadia squeezed my arm. "Oh, sweetie. Don't give up. I know George wasn't the right one, but I really do think the list works. I say we start fresh."

The last thing I was going to do was let Dr. Susie

mess up another relationship. No way. Mom squeezed my arm. When I looked over at her, she pointed up. There, standing on the stage near the *Wake Up Denver* hosts, was Robert. My stomach grew tight. I glanced at Mom. I didn't have to say a word. She'd known all this time I'd come to the festival searching for him. Wow, he looked so good. Handsome, freshly shaven, his dark hair perfectly swept up off his forehead. How I'd missed him.

"Nadia, I think I know what I want now." I turned to look at Mom. "Really." Mom's face broke into a giddy smile. She could read me like a book. "I'll catch you guys later." I sprinted away from Mom and Nadia, even as Nadia opened her mouth to say something.

"Let her go," I heard Mom tell Nadia as I pushed my way through the thick crowd to the platform stage. I moved across the street, nearly being run over by a big red-and-gold dragon as I ducked and weaved through the parade. I momentarily lost Robert. He'd moved from the stage. *No! Where'd he go?*

"Find your spot," Cissy chimed in from the stage. No Robert in sight. I'd just seen him. I moved past a burly drummer and a flute player. I looked right and left, but no sign of him. He'd disappeared in the crowd.

"Raise your lanterns," Kyle called. A sea of people raised white lanterns, some of them already lit and ready to go. Next to me, someone lifted a big white lantern and I found myself just twenty feet from Robert. I sprinted the rest of the way to him, though he hadn't seen me. He was intent on lighting his own lantern.

"And here we go!" Cissy cried. "In ten, nine, eight, seven, six, five, four..."

I made it to Robert but accidentally bumped straight into him, causing him to lose hold of his lantern. It floated up early, even as Cissy's countdown hit zero, and the rest of the lanterns lifted up into the sky.

"Happy New Year!" everyone shouted.

"Hey," I said, as Robert watched his lantern float up ahead of the rest and then looked at me uncertainly.

"Hey," Robert said, voice laced with caution. I guess I deserved that. I hadn't been all that nice to him the last time we met.

"I was hoping I'd find you here," I said.

"Here I am," Robert said, shoving his hands into his pockets. He glanced away from me as if looking for an exit. *No, no, no.* I had to make this right.

"I made a *huge* mistake," I said, clutching the sherpa lapel of his coat. "And I...misjudged you. And, truthfully, I shouldn't have been judging you at all. I should have been getting to know you instead of applying these ridiculous guidelines—" My mouth was on autopilot, and I didn't even know what I was saying.

"What are you talking about?" Robert looked genuinely confused.

"You're full of surprises, and you're fun, and you're thoughtful, and I just wanted you to know I was wrong."

Robert still looked wary. Not that I blamed him. I'd been Lucy with that darn football since we'd started dating. Every time he'd gotten close enough to kick it, I'd ripped it out from under him, and like Charlie Brown, he'd gone flying. I'd been so very unfair.

"Cass, what do you want from me?" he asked.

"I know that I don't deserve a second chance, but I really hope you give me one." I swallowed the lump in my throat. It was now or never. "I guess what I'm trying to say is…"

His dark eyes studied me, and in that moment, words failed me. Because words weren't what I needed right now. I stood on tiptoes and kissed him on the lips. Better to show him how I felt than talk about it. Besides, I always hated talking about feelings.

The kiss was as electric as the kiss in the bowling alley. He kissed me back with just as much passion, as I pressed my lips against his. Who needed a coat? My whole body was suddenly on fire. Sparks? This was a raging inferno. I broke free at last, and a bevy of fireworks exploded above our heads. At first, I thought it was just Robert's amazing charisma, and then I realized it was part of the festival. Robert seemed speechless, too. Did he feel the same way about me? He'd kissed me back. I'd felt it. He'd wanted that kiss as much as I did.

"I'm also really sorry that I bumped into you and made you let your lantern go," I said.

"That's okay. I'll let the lantern go," he said and then he pulled me into his arms. "Because I'm holding on to you."

"Hmmmmm…" I groaned.

"So cheesy?" he finished.

"Sooooo cheesy." I giggled, enjoying Robert's warm arms around me. I knew now that true love was worth the risk. Everything was perfect with the world. Wait…one thing was missing. I looked up at Robert, and he pulled me close, kissing me once more.

Now everything was truly and absolutely right with the world, right here in Robert's arms.

Epilogue

Two Years Later

NADIA WAS IN RARE FORM as she flipped through her big white binder and also managed to somehow hold on to her squirming almost-two-year-old on one hip. Miya had been a handful ever since she'd been born. She hated naptimes and *schedules.* She was a girl after my own heart. I grinned at her, and she smiled back.

"Let me just double check the *list*," Nadia said, glancing at the paper. "We've got the musicians, *check,* the cake delivered, *check.*" She glanced at me. "*The bride,* check."

"Nadia, it'll be fine. You can put down the binder." I flattened the skirt of my white sheath satin gown, even as I worried the train behind me might get tangled somehow on my way down the aisle.

Nadia shook her head furiously. "I don't want you to end up like *my* wedding." Her toddler kept squirming harder, trying to reach the ground, not caring how her struggles wrinkled her flower girl dress. I knew from experience that once she hit the floor, my niece would be off like a shot.

"I can hold her," I offered, but Nadia nearly dropped the binder.

"You're wearing *white*." She sounded appalled. "She'd destroy that dress!"

I glanced in the full-length mirror at my white sheath of a wedding dress, decorated with lace trim. We were in the tiny upstairs dressing room in the small chapel where my mom and dad had gotten married. I thought I should be nervous on my wedding day, but I wasn't. Not at all. I couldn't wait to say *I do,* which said quite a lot coming from *this* little commitment-phobe.

A soft knock came at the door. "Is everyone decent?" Michael's voice came through the oak paneled door.

"Yes," I called and Michael peeked in, Jeremy by his side.

"Whoa, Cass! You look great." Michael nodded, like an approving big brother. I wanted to twirl around so he could see the back, but I was still worried about the train.

"We're ready in five minutes," he said. "Can I help?"

"Take Miya, please," Nadia begged as she handed her wiggly little girl to her husband.

"Who's my little girl?" Michael said. He gently put Miya on the ground, but in a split second, she ran off. Jeremy trotted after her.

"Michael!" hissed Nadia, looking at the ceiling in frustration.

"I've got them," Michael said, on the case. "No! Not the stairs! Miya!" A bit of panic crept into Michael's voice. Nadia palmed her forehead.

"It's okay," I said. "How much damage can they do?"

Nadia laughed ruefully. "A lot." She shook her head at me. "You *sure* you want to do this? Be married… have kids… You could learn from my mistakes." One of her eyebrows quirked up.

I laughed. "I'm sure," I said, thinking of Robert and his warm brown eyes. We'd spent the last two years of dating feeling like we were two halves of the same person. Getting married wouldn't change that. Not in the least. Organ music wafted up from downstairs. I felt a tiny little prick of nerves in my stomach. Not because I was worried about getting married. No, I knew I'd finally found what Mom and Dad had, and I couldn't wait to spend the rest of my life with Robert. Mom came around the corner and when she saw me through the open door, tears sprang to her eyes.

"Cass! You look...beautiful," she sniffed as she came over and gave me a gentle hug. "So...beautiful. Oh, how I wish your dad was here to see this."

Me too. "I think he's here in spirit."

"I know, wherever he is, he approves," Mom said. She pressed a crumpled up tissue against her nose.

"Now, don't cry," scolded Nadia, sniffling too. "Or you'll make me cry. And then we'll have one big mascara mess."

I hugged them both. Nadia glanced at her watch. "It's time," she murmured. "It's time!" She clutched the big white wedding binder to her chest. "Okay, you remember that Miya goes, then Jeremy and then me, and then you and Mom..."

"Yes, we know. I'll be walking her down the aisle," Mom said.

"Oh! The flower girl basket," Nadia cried, as if she'd forgotten to turn off the oven.

"It'll be fine, Nadia," I called after her as she scurried down the stairs.

Mom helped me adjust my veil and wrangled my train into submission, and then she offered me her arm. It seemed right, somehow. We walked down the staircase and hung out at the back of the chapel, which was full-to-bursting with a hundred and thirty of our closest friends and family.

The processional music began and then my niece

bolted down the aisle, dropping her flower basket. The crowd laughed. She then stuck her thumb in her mouth as Nadia rushed down the aisle after her, trying to get her out of the way. Jeremy came next, my ring bearer.

Then came the music for the bride. I'd opted not to use traditional music. Instead, I'd picked Mom's favorite song, in instrumental form, "I Can't Fight This Feeling Any Longer." Somehow, even on a chapel organ, it sounded right.

Mom squeezed my arm as everyone stood and we began our walk down the aisle. But I fixed my gaze on Robert, devilishly handsome in his black tuxedo. He was everything I wanted in a partner: funny, smart, considerate, and the last two years had taught me that relationships could get better with time. I couldn't wait to see what the future held for us. A house? Kids? I hoped so. Life was short and unpredictable, true, but I promised myself to enjoy every minute I had with Robert. And no matter what, I'd never let a TV personality make major life decisions for me again. If I'd learned one lesson, it was to trust my instincts.

I glanced up and saw Dana waving wildly at me from the fifth pew, looking every bit as happy as the day she'd become Mrs. Schmointz. Of course, even the pew couldn't hide her growing belly. Pretty soon, there'd be a baby Schmointz in the mix and I couldn't wait to meet him or her.

I glanced back at Robert and he winked at me, and I felt right at ease. I could marry him every day for the rest of my life, I thought. I realized I'd only been worried about commitment before because I hadn't met the right man yet.

At the end of the aisle, Mom let me go with a kiss on the cheek as she swiped a tear from her face. She also gave Robert a huge hug, to the joy of the crowd, and then bustled off to her seat. I could feel Dad smiling down on me from heaven. I knew he'd approve. Robert took my hand.

"Are we going to have to say something about sharing food in the vows?" he murmured in my ear.

"Oh, you bet. To share till we part," I whispered and he chuckled, a low growl.

"I have a feeling I'm not going to get any wedding cake, am I?" He grinned.

I squeezed his hand in mine as I thought about the three-layer sweets-monster fantasy cake that awaited us at our reception. I giggled to myself. "Probably not."

"As long as I have you, I couldn't care less."

A man who'd let me have *all* the wedding cake? Now I knew for sure: this was true love.

Lemon Elderflower Mini Bundt Cakes

A Hallmark Original Recipe

In *Dater's Handbook*, Cass has an "inner sweets monster" that can't be tamed. The fun-loving Robert indulges it, while the sophisticated George disapproves. Could there be a clearer indication of which man is right for her? Our Lemon Elderflower Mini Bundt Cakes are refined enough for any taste, and would tempt anyone to steal an extra bite.

Yield: 12 Mini Bundt Cakes
Prep Time: 60 minutes

Bake Time: 20 minutes
Total Time: 80 minutes

INGREDIENTS

Mini Bundt Cakes:
- 2 cups Greek yogurt
- 1/4 cup plus 2 tablespoons elderflower syrup*
- 2 lemons, zested and juiced
- 3 1/3 cups flour
- 2 teaspoons baking soda
- 1/2 teaspoon salt
- 2 sticks (1 cup) unsalted butter, at room temperature
- 2 cups granulated sugar
- 4 large eggs, room temperature

Glaze:
- 1/2 cup powdered sugar
- 1 tablespoon elderflower syrup*
- 1 tablespoon fresh squeezed lemon juice

Lemon Elderflower Buttercream (optional)
- 1 stick (1/2 cup) unsalted butter, at room temperature
- 2 cups powdered sugar
- 2 tablespoons fresh squeezed lemon juice
- 1 tablespoon elderflower syrup*

*Elderflower syrup (such as Norm's Farms), elderflower cordial or elderflower liqueur (such as St Germain) can all be used interchangeably for this recipe. Elderflower syrup is called elderflower cordial in the UK. Contrary to the name, the cordial does not contain alcohol. Both elderflower syrup and elderflower cordial are easy to source on line and are available at health food and specialty grocery stores. Elderflower liqueur is widely available in larger liquor stores. To prepare elderflower liqueur syrup, combine equal parts elderflower liqueur and sugar in saucepan, heat until sugar is dissolved and cool.

DIRECTIONS

1. To prepare bundt cakes: Preheat oven to 350 degrees. Coat two 6-cake mini bundt cake pans with nonstick cooking spray.

2. In a medium bowl, combine yogurt, 1/4 cup elderflower syrup, lemon zest and juice; whisk to blend. Set aside. In another medium bowl, sift together flour, baking powder and salt; set aside.

3. In a bowl with electric mixer, cream butter and sugar until light and fluffy. Add eggs one at a time; mix well. Add reserved yogurt and flour

mixtures alternately to mixer bowl and beat until blended.

4. Spoon batter into prepared pans, filling 3/4 full. Bake for 17 to 20 minutes, or until golden and a toothpick inserted in cakes comes out clean. Cool for 10 minutes; invert on wire rack to release cakes. Brush cakes lightly with 2 tablespoons elderflower syrup.

5. To prepare glaze: Combine powdered sugar, elderflower syrup and lemon juice in bowl; whisk. Drizzle over cooled bundt cakes.

6. To prepare buttercream (optional): Combine butter, powdered sugar, lemon juice and elderflower syrup in mixer bowl; beat on medium speed until light and fluffy. Pipe or spoon frosting in the center of glazed bundt cakes.

Thanks so much for reading *Dater's Handbook*.
We hope you enjoyed it!

You might also like these other ebooks
from Hallmark Publishing:

Journey Back to Christmas
Christmas in Homestead
Love You Like Christmas
A Heavenly Christmas
A Dash of Love
Moonlight in Vermont
Like Cats and Dogs

For information about our new releases and
exclusive offers, sign up for our free newsletter!

You can also connect with us here:

Facebook.com/HallmarkPublishing

Twitter.com/HallmarkPublish

Country Wedding

Leigh Duncan

Chapter One

BRADLEY SUTTONS TWIRLED HIS STETSON on the tips of his fingers. Light glinted off the buckle on the fourteen-hundred-dollar hat that had been a gift from his agent. In the shadows beyond the cameras that tracked his every move, someone made a chopping motion, meaning *Stop that.*

Bradley stilled. He traced his fingers over the brim and gave himself a stern reminder to keep his trademark smile in place while he willed away the urge to squint or squirm or stand and walk straight out of the studio.

Quit your bellyaching. He wasn't really going to complain about the dizzying heat or the blinding glow that came from all the spotlights aimed at him, was he? Not when he'd spent the past ten years working to get where he was. Every step he'd taken, every stage he'd stepped onto in the bars around Nashville, every mic he'd poured his heart and soul into—they'd all led to this moment.

He glanced at the incredibly talented, beautiful woman seated next to him on the couch. Catherine tipped her head toward his. The smile she always wore in public, the one that rarely touched eyes the color of fine cognac, deepened as she met his gaze. A long, blonde curl slid over her shoulder. Bradley's fingers ached to reach out, tuck the errant hair back into place. Aware that millions of viewers were watching, he merely cupped his knee. He was a lucky, lucky man. He'd landed the girl of his dreams, signed a recording contract, amassed a fortune, and now, finally, had the fame that guaranteed the fulfillment of his every wish. Not too bad for a kid whose whole world had come tumbling down around him at thirteen.

The final chorus of "Love Don't Die Easy" bounced off the walls of the studio. He looked up as the hit that had catapulted him into stardom came to an end.

"I love that song." The host of the nation's most popular morning talk show tapped his fingers on the armrest of his chair. Seated to give viewers the full benefit of the panoramic view of Hollywood over his shoulder, Stan beamed a dreamy smile straight into the cameras. "How did it feel to win Album Of The Year at the Grammys?"

Surreal. Bradley glanced down at the toes of his shoes. The Italian leather boots probably cost more than he'd earned in the entire year he'd written that song. He leaned forward, directing his answer at the blinking red light on Camera Three rather than their host, just like Catherine had coached him to do. "Well, not too long ago I was playing in bars and clubs around Nashville. So, winning a Grammy has been quite a change." Thanks to the award, he had the life that, a few years ago, he'd only dreamed of living.

Not that everything was perfect. All the newfound fame and fortune had placed so many extra demands on his time that he was way behind on the new album. Between his schedule and Catherine's work on what was sure to be another blockbuster movie, the two of them rarely spent any time alone together. When she'd called last night and asked if he could free up his morning, he'd had a momentary vision of the two of them eating breakfast and trading kisses over orange juice and coffee. Instead, they'd spent the last two hours in makeup and rehearsals before they were ushered onto the set.

But no one turned down the opportunity to appear on Stan's show. No one. Not unless they wanted to watch their careers sink below the horizon like the setting sun. Careful not to let even the slightest hint of frustration show, Bradley eased back into the plush leather couch when the host's attention shifted.

"Catherine Mann." Stan's dark eyes lit with the fervor of a true fan. The coppery brackets around his mouth deepened as, exuding confidence and poise, he crossed one long leg over the other. "It's a real thrill to have you in the studio today."

"Thank you, Stan." Catherine's perfectly modulated voice caressed the mics while she gave the shy smile that had first delighted movie goers when she was a child, turned her name into a household word as a teen, and stolen his heart the moment Bradley had met her. "It's a pleasure to be here."

"You discovered Bradley, didn't you?" The consummate morning show host, Stan dove straight into the meat of the interview. "I mean, he was already well known in Nashville. But you brought him to Los Angeles and got him a recording deal."

Bradley felt his shoulders stiffen. Sure, things had begun to change for him once he and Catherine had started seeing each other. Her name had opened a few doors. But it had been his talent that had propelled him upward and gotten him where he was today.

"I introduced him to a few people," Catherine admitted. She slipped her perfectly manicured fingers over his knee and stared deeply into his eyes. "But he's a pretty talented guy. He got himself a recording deal."

Her firm answer shut down Stan's line of questioning and soothed the acidic burn in Bradley's stomach. Undaunted, the talk show host smoothly changed subjects. "And the two of you have been inseparable ever since?"

The melodic tones of Catherine's laugh echoed through the small space. "I think the first time I heard Bradley sing"—emotion flickered in her eyes for an all-too-brief moment before she turned to face Stan—"I fell in love with him."

As if he sensed a story, Stan leaned forward. "Are you saying the two of you might have some news for us one day?"

Bradley straightened and said, "We like to keep our private lives private." In rehearsals, Stan had offered repeated assurances that his guests' personal lives would remain off-limits. Yet less than five minutes into the interview, the host was already prying into matters Bradley and Catherine had decided they'd rather not have aired on national TV. He looked to Catherine for support.

"We're engaged to be married," his bride-to-be blurted.

Despite the countless stage appearances and a thousand-and-one coaching sessions where he'd learned to keep a carefully crafted façade in place, Bradley couldn't even begin to hide his surprise.

He and Catherine had talked about this. They'd decided to keep the depth of their feelings for one another hidden from their adoring—but demanding—fans who'd insist on knowing every detail of their wedding plans. She knew how important it was to him to keep their relationship to themselves. So why had she just shared the news of their engagement on national TV?

"Now, I know we agreed not to share this publicly, but..." Catherine patted his arm. The wattage on her signature smile increased to the point where it practically guaranteed to turn her fans' hearts all aflutter. "I just want the whole world to know how happy I am."

"Well, you heard it here first, folks." Stan's pleased grin announced to viewers everywhere that he'd just scored the scoop of the century. "Catherine Mann and Bradley Suttons are engaged to be married!"

Bradley took a deep breath, steadied his nerves, and aimed a loving look at his fiancée. There really wasn't anything else for him to do, was there? He couldn't very well shut the door now that the horse had already bolted out of the barn. Besides, if he knew anything about his fiancée, it was that Catherine never made a move in public without having a very good reason for it.

Now, he just needed to figure out what that reason was.

Sarah Standor dusted her hands on the back of her well-worn jeans as the screened door she'd been walking in and out of her entire life swung shut behind her. Voices came from the corner of the roomy ranch house. She'd left the TV on to keep her rescue dogs company while she fed and watered the horses this morning. When she glanced at the screen, her footsteps slowed.

The devastatingly handsome cowboy on the talk show sat next to Catherine Mann, America's reigning box-office queen. Sarah resumed her march to the coffeemaker and poured herself a much-needed cup. The starlet on TV giggled like a schoolgirl, tossed her long blonde curls, and announced their engagement. The groom-to-be looked as if he'd just swallowed a canary.

Sarah shook her head and laughed. *Bradley Suttons.* Along with every other person who lived within a fifty-mile radius, she'd followed the meteoric rise of Mill Town's favorite son. It didn't seem to matter to anyone that Bradley had moved clear across the country when he was thirteen and never once returned for a visit. Or that the house he'd lived in as a child had sat vacant all these years. The good citizens of the town and surrounding areas had claimed him as their own, and that was that.

And now, he was engaged to be married to Catherine Mann, America's sweetheart. Talk about power couples. Their union was sure to top all the Who's Who lists from Nashville to Hollywood, and everywhere in between.

"Well, congratulations, Brad-Bird." Sarah smiled.

A noise from the other end of the house interrupted before she'd finished doctoring her coffee with cream and sugar. She glanced down the hallway that ran as straight as a shotgun from the back door to the front of the house. A familiar figure stood on the wide porch. Sarah noted the suit and tie the banker wore beneath his Stetson and sighed. She'd hoped to put off the inevitable just a little while longer, but it looked like the day she'd been dreading had arrived. Forcing a cheery note into her voice, she called, "Mornin' James."

"Mornin'." Without waiting for an invitation, James let himself in.

"What brings you out here so early?" Sarah took a steadying breath and prepared for the worst. She'd known she couldn't dodge the banker forever. In a place the size of Mill Town, there really wasn't anywhere to hide.

"Well, I had to come out here to see you since you

won't answer any of my phone calls or emails." His boot heels rattling against the hardwood floors, James swept the wide-brimmed hat from his head and ran a hand over his sparse hair.

Sarah propped one hand on the kitchen table and leaned on it for support. She was pretty sure she was going to need it. Still, it wouldn't do to let the banker see her sweat. Not quite sure how she did it, she managed a teasing smile. "Well, I don't got time for phone calls and emails. I got a ranch to run." Hoping she'd guessed wrong about her visitor's intentions, she asked, "How's your mama?"

"She's...she's real good." His expression far too serious for a social call, James moved closer.

"She get those garden roses I sent over?" It really was a shame that her boarding stables didn't produce revenue as well as her flowers did. When it came to those, she was known throughout the county for her green thumb. She grabbed the remote control and turned down the volume on the television set.

"She did, and I thank you." James rocked his hat back and forth, talking with his Stetson like people back East spoke with their hands.

"She is such a sweet lady." Uncertain how much longer she could stall, Sarah sipped from her mug. "James, you want some coffee?"

"I'd love a half a cup of coffee." James parked his

hat on the kitchen table. He rubbed one finger down his equine nose and straightened the strings of his bolo tie. "But you need to quit changing the subject, 'cause we need to talk about your finances."

Sarah heard the frustration in his voice. It pained her to put her friend in such an awkward spot, but what else was she supposed to do?

She'd grown up in this house. She knew every creaking floorboard. She knew the way to twist the handle in the shower to coax the most hot water from the ancient boiler, and that she could cool the entire house by propping open the front and back doors on a summer's evening.

Still, even though the ranch had been in her family for generations, she could've walked away from it if she only had herself to think about. But there was far more to it than that. If she lost the ranch, what would become of the horses she cared for? Of the dogs she'd rescued and who now served as her surrogate family? Who would tend to the gardens that provided flowers for weddings and funerals and high school proms and, yes, brought such joy to people like James's mother?

She couldn't lose the ranch. She just couldn't. The ugly fact was, though, she didn't have the money to pay off all her debts.

Hoping to stall, she resorted to the one thing that had worked so far—she hedged. "Now, my mama told me never to talk about politics or money in mixed company," she said as she poured James's coffee and topped off her own cup.

"There's no getting around this, Sarah." James held out his empty palms. "I'm going to have to foreclose on you and sell off this ranch if you can't find a way to make the mortgage payments. If it were up to me—"

"It is up to you, Jimmy." With more firmness than she'd intended, she handed him his cup. "You're the president of Mill Town Bank."

James's voice rose in protest. "I don't *own* the bank, Sarah."

Her shoulders slumped. As desperate as she was to hold onto the ranch, she wouldn't beg, wouldn't put her childhood friend in an awkward position.

One final chance existed to salvage her situation. She crossed her fingers. "I'm just waiting to hear if I got this grant from the Equine Rehabilitation Fund." With the money from the foundation, she'd be able to bring her mortgage up to date and buy enough feed and hay to see her stock through the winter. Without it, though... She stopped her train of thought. She had to get that grant. She had to.

James's voice dropped to a near whisper. "I've given you six months more than I have any right to, and now I have no choice."

Sarah stared at the floor. She'd exhausted all her

other options. The Equine Rehabilitation Fund was her last hope. They'd already had her application for far too long, but any day now, they had to approve her request and send the money she needed. She lifted her head and looked James in the eye. "One month," she pleaded. "That's all I'm asking."

A long minute stretched out while she held her breath and prayed. At last, the bank president held up a finger. "One month, Sarah. That takes us to June first."

Deliberately, she straightened her shoulders. James was going pretty far out on a weak limb to give her this last chance to balance her accounts. She had to make sure he didn't regret it. "I will tell you what," she began. "If I don't have the money by June first, I will walk into your office, I will shake your hand, and I will sign this ranch over to you."

"Well, that's—that's fair." To free up his right hand, James shifted his coffee mug into his left.

Sarah took the hand he extended and gave it a firm shake. "You need me to sign something?"

James lifted the hand she'd just shaken. "You just did."

Sarah hefted her mug. A warmth that had nothing to do with the coffee she swigged spread through her midsection. Despite all her financial woes, returning to Mill Town after graduation had been the right decision. Where else would the president of the bank do business on a handshake?

The reason for his visit concluded, James pointed over her shoulder to the television where the morning talk show had continued. "That guy grew up here," he announced.

Sarah took a second to swallow her coffee. "Bradley Suttons." She nodded. "He used to live next door. Moved away when he was about thirteen. But I believe he still owns the house."

"I remember." Sympathy tugged at the corners of James's lips. "His parents were killed in that car accident over in Greenbrier."

"Yep." Propping her elbow on the arm she'd folded across her chest, she tipped her coffee cup toward the screen. She'd never known there was such sadness in the world before the day that word of the Suttons' deaths spread through the town. But, as bad as their loss had been for her, it had been so much worse for the boy next door. One minute, her best friend had been a normal kid growing up in a small town with his whole future laid out for him. The next, everything he'd ever known—his parents, his home, his friends— had been stripped away from him.

"He must be about the most famous resident to ever come out of Mill Town." James lifted one eyebrow. "I guess you knew him pretty well?"

"Knew him?" She took a long swallow from her mug. "I was married to him."

Later that evening, she still chuckled at the mix of confusion and surprise that had filled James's face when she'd announced her marriage to Bradley Suttons. Only three people knew of the ceremony that had taken place in her parents' barn that day. She'd never spoken of it. She was pretty sure none of the others had, either. They'd only been thirteen, after all. And anyway, a mere twenty-four hours later, Bradley's aunt and uncle had whisked him off to Nashville to start his new life.

In the bedroom she'd decorated with hand-me-downs and items she'd found at tag sales, she tugged an old wooden box from beneath the wrought iron bed. Layers of quilts and blankets sank beneath her as she settled onto the mattress and lifted the lid of the treasure box her dad had made. Leather hinges creaked. She drank in the scent of old paper, aged cedar, and memories.

Setting aside the colored pencil drawing that had taken first place in the eighth grade art show, she thumbed through the stacks of ribbons she'd won in riding competitions, the report cards filled with A's, the awards. Her fingertips brushed against velvety softness. There it was, tucked into the corner, right where she'd put it all those years ago. She retrieved the small cloth bag and loosened the drawstring. A diamond solitaire fell into the palm of her hand when she upended the pouch. She held the ring up to the light and smiled, remembering the day she'd wed Bradley Suttons.

When she couldn't find her best friend anywhere in the house crowded with people and hothouse flowers, she'd somehow known he'd be in the old barn. Careful not to ruin her best dress, she'd climbed the rickety ladder into the loft. There, amid the dust motes that danced in the beams of sunlight that seeped through cracks in the barn's wood-slatted walls, she'd found him. He'd been sitting alone, his tightly pressed lips wobbling, his chin tucked down like a bird with a broken wing. She'd plopped down on a bale of hay left over from the previous winter and faced him.

"It's okay to cry, Brad-Bird. I won't tell anyone," she'd promised. Anyone who'd lost his parents was allowed a few tears.

But Bradley hadn't cried. He hadn't even looked up from the shiny surface of his leather shoes. "I can't believe I have to move away from here."

"It'll be fine. You're so smart and everything." She wished she could think of something that would help his heart heal.

"Guess I'm sort of an orphan now. I don't really have a family anymore."

That had to be the worst. The entire Standor family—her grandparents, aunts, uncles and a whole passel of cousins—all lived within walking distance. But Bradley only had one aunt and uncle, and they lived clear across the country in Tennessee. By this time next week, he'd be living with them in a house he'd never seen before, attending classes in a school where he didn't know a soul. She had to do something—anything—to make it better for him, but what?

"Hey." His footsteps heavy, their friend Adam slowly trudged up the stairs to join them. Behind him, loose hay sifted onto the floor below. "I was looking for you guys."

Suddenly, she knew. "Let's get married."

"What?" The look Bradley gave her said she'd lost her mind.

"We should get married." The idea had come to her out of the blue, but it made perfect sense. "Then, we can be each other's family."

Though some of the sadness faded from Bradley's eyes, he shook his head. "We're only thirteen. We can't get married."

"Yes, we can. This is my barn, so I make the rules." She glanced around. From the tack draped across the stair rail to the bales of hay to the sunlight that streamed in through the big sliding door on the ground floor, she knew every inch of the barn as well as she knew the freckles on her arms. She'd raised puppies in the back stall, had taken her first pony ride down the wide middle aisle, felt the velvety noses of her dad's racehorses when she fed them apple slices. The barn was her kingdom, and she dared anyone to tell her what she could or couldn't do in it. Getting married to Bradley was the right thing to do. "You're my best friend, and I say we can do anything we want."

"How are we supposed to get married?" A faint trace of interest crept into Bradley's voice.

"I can marry you." Adam's gaze swung between his two friends. "My dad's a pastor. I've seen him do it, like, a hundred times. It's not that hard."

One look at the hope that gleamed in Bradley's eyes banished all her doubts. Her best friend needed a family. What better way to give him one than for them to get married? Wasn't family what marriage was all about?

Shaking off thoughts from long ago, Sarah slipped the ring onto the fourth finger of her left hand and admired how the light glinted off the diamond. Not that she had any intention of keeping it. She grabbed a sheet of stationery and a pen from the roll-top desk where, among other things, she'd written a dozen letters to the Equine Rehabilitation Fund. Though

Bradley's ring had to be worth a sizeable amount, maybe even enough to settle all her debts, it wasn't hers. Not really. The ring belonged to a boy she'd once loved enough to marry. That boy was gone now. He'd grown into a man who'd gotten himself engaged to Catherine Mann. And, without giving herself a chance to reconsider, Sarah began to write.

Country Wedding *is coming soon from Hallmark Publishing!*